Madame Bulldog struck ⸻
and grabbed Wallace's gun ⸻
turned swiftly as the man recovered and prepared to resume
his attack. 'I can copper that bet, too!' she warned, cocking
the revolver. Looking down the Colt's muzzle, the man froze,
every instinct warning him that the new owner of the Hide
and Horn Saloon was perfectly capable of handling a gun—
and would have no hestitation in doing so.

THE HIDE AND HORN SALOON

List of **J.T.** EDSON *titles in chronological and categorical sequence.*

THE HIDE AND
HORN SALOON

J.T. EDSON

CORGI BOOKS

THE HIDE AND HORN SALOON
A CORGI BOOK 0 552 12192 4

First publication in Great Britain
PRINTING HISTORY
Corgi edition published 1983

This book is set in 10 pt. Palatino

Corgi Books are published by Transworld Publishers Ltd.,
Century House, 61-63 Uxbridge Road,
Ealing, London W5 5SA

Printed and bound in Great Britain by
Cox & Wyman Ltd, Reading

For my good friend Pam Brett, who always beats me at golf—she keeps the score, you see—and her daughter, Vickie, who finds my lost balls—at fifty pence a time.

THE HIDE AND HORN SALOON

Author's note:

WHILE complete in itself, this title precedes the events recorded in: CUT ONE, THEY ALL BLEED. Some of the events recorded in both volumes previously appeared under the title, Part One, 'Better Than Calamity', THE WILD-CATS. However, the Counter family have agreed that the full story can at last be put into print. They made a stipulation that the two books must be included in the Calamity Jane and not the Floating Outfit series, as was the case formerly, which we have done.

To save our 'old hands' from repetition, but for the benefit of new readers, we have given information about various references to incidents and explained those Old West terms about which we are mostly regularly asked in the form of an Appendix.

We realise that in our present 'permissive' society, we could include the actual profanities used by various people in the narrative, but we do not concede that a spurious desire for 'realism' is any excuse to do so.

Lastly, as we do not pander to the current 'trendy' usage of the metric system, except where the calibres of certain firearms—i.e., Walther P-38, 9mm—are concerned, we will continue to employ miles, yards, feet, inches, pounds and ounces, when referring to distances and weights.

J.T. EDSON
Active Member, Western Writers of America
Melton Mowbray,
Leics.,
England.

CHAPTER ONE

A Real Tough Place

The arrival of a stagecoach was considered to be something of an event in any small or medium sized town west of the Mississippi River that was fortunate enough to be the recipient of such a service.

Certainly Tennyson, in Sand County, Texas, was no exception!

With the twice weekly stagecoach being due, much the same crowd as usual was gathered in the immediate vicinity of the Wells Fargo office and depot just after one o'clock that warm early spring afternoon. Prominent was a proportion of local businessmen, ostensibly present to find out whether small items they had ordered were aboard. A number of genuine loafers, inevitably, were on hand, some of whom belonged to that section of the community which existed either with no visible means of support, or by taking occasional forms of casual employment. Others were cowhands from the surrounding ranches, paying a visit during what a later generation would call a 'day off'. Having nothing of greater importance demanding their attention, all were hoping the passengers on the stagecoach would be interesting and offer a subject for conversation.

Several of Tennyson's 'good' women invariably attended each arrival, anxious to preserve their upright and God-fearing community and conscious of the town's growing prosperity and further expansion. Like their menfolk, sober citizens all, they regarded the present status of their township with mixed feelings. They considered that having been accepted as a recognized stop on a major stage route was proof of the social prominence acquired by Tennyson. Nevertheless, this also emphasised a sense of injustice over the town of Garnett which was no larger than Tennyson but which—as result of legal shenanigans on the part of certain 'carpetbagger' politicians with business connections there—had been appointed 'seat' of Sand County. However, 'Reconstruction' was in the process of being brought to an end. The hated rule of Governor Bartholemew Davis would soon be over and it was hoped the elected dignitary who replaced him might be persuaded to redress the situation. Therefore, with such a desirable end in mind, members of the Ladies Guild For Civic Betterment felt it incumbent upon themselves to ensure no undesirable persons should arrive with the intention of taking up even temporary residence in their community.

However, in one respect, the presence and scrutiny of the 'good' women was a needless precaution!

Equally aware of the need to present a suitably law abiding image, although the term was not yet in popular usage and expressing it in such a fashion would never have occurred to him, Town Marshal Tune Collier always took measures which were intended to prevent any unsavoury characters invading his bailiwick.[1] But on this occasion, as other matters were demanding his attention, his deputy was standing in

1. *When producing the manuscript for* Part One, 'Better Than Calamity'. THE WILDCATS, *we were led to assume by our source of information that the surname of the town marshal was 'Counter'. However, Andrew Mark 'Big Andy' Counter has asked that we correct this misapprehension and, as we do in* CUT ONE, THEY ALL BLEED, *use Tune Collier's real name. J.T.E.*

the background at a point which offered an unrestricted view of the arrival area.

Medium height, stocky, white haired, walrus moustached and leathery featured, with grin quirks at the corners of eyes little dimmed by the passage of time, Deputy Town Marshal Herman 'Pockets' Hoscroft could have passed for one of the genuine loafers if it had not been for two things. One was the well polished badge of office on his black and white calfskin vest, the other, the Greener ten gauge shotgun resting its twenty inch long twin barrels with apparent negligence across the crook of his bent left arm—the latter augmenting the walnut handled Colt 1860 Army Model revolver in the open topped holster of his Confederate States' cavalry style gunbelt. Apart from these indications of his true status, his attire was that of a not too prosperous Texas' cowhand. Appearances notwithstanding, and regardless of having long since passed the first flush of youth, he was fully capable of enforcing a suggestion that an incoming passenger might be happier elsewhere and he had no need to call upon the assistance of the 'good' women, nor his superior in most cases, to support him.

A surge of anticipation, far greater than would have manifested itself in regions of greater sophistication, swept through the assembled spectators as the stagecoach came into view over the not too distant horizon. It was no mere 'mud wagon' making a connection to a main stage route, but a full blown Concord with a six-horse team and offering all the style of its superlative class of transport.[2] Not only did it bring in the United States' mail, but a certain amount of freight could also be carried; including, on occasion, items of considerable value in the strongbox carried beneath the driver's seat. Nevertheless, it was the passengers

2. *Descriptions of two different types of 'Concord' stagecoaches can be found in:* WACO'S BADGE *and* CALAMITY SPELLS TROUBLE. *J.T.E.*

who aroused the interest of the waiting people rather than the load. In addition to the possibility of there being travellers of some consequence aboard, even the humblest passengers bore news of events elsewhere which would not otherwise have reached the town until much later by conventional means.

To be strictly truthful, up to that time no person of any consequence had ever visited, nor even passed through, Tennyson. The famous names of the theatrical and entertainment world never came to display their respective talents. Nor, particularly with the population disfranchised as a result of Texas having supported the right of any State to secede from the Union (if finding its interests incompatible with those of the Federal Government) had any prominent politician as yet considered it might prove worth his while to arrive and explain his policies in the hope of acquiring the votes of the citizens. Neither had any of the gun fighters whose names had become legendary, nor members of the ranching business, put in an appearance by stagecoach, or any other kind of transportation. Furthermore, as the town had never attained a reputation for offering games of chance with high stakes—often a most lucrative source of added income even to businesses not directly involved— noted professional gamblers never felt inclined to include it in their itineraries.

Regardless of all this, goaded by 'the hope which springs eternal within the human breast', the various onlookers invariably forgathered in case the situation might change for the better.

To all appearances, on its arrival, the latest stage-coach seemed unlikely to offer any significant alteration to the pattern!

The only passenger was a woman!

However, although the solitary passenger alighted and was clearly waiting for her baggage to be unloaded, almost everybody present realized she was a stranger to Tennyson!

Five foot five in height, the woman looked to be in her late thirties or early forties. A small and dainty Wavelean hat sat impaled by a pin to piled up blonde hair which the 'good' ladies, although the conclusion perhaps resulted from feminine cattiness towards one much better favoured physically than themselves, whispered to one another had acquired its hue by artificial means. While not exactly out and out beautiful in the classic sense, her features were attractive, with full lips which were clearly used to merriment and yet also gave a hint of a very strong personality. They, and her cheeks, had just enough make-up to be acceptable by the social standards of the town, even to the most discerning observers of her own sex. Stylish and costly, her dove grey two-piece travelling costume and frilly bosomed light blue silk blouse were in just as excellent taste. The black gloves she was wearing prevented her marital status from being exhibited, but the small amount of jewellery she was displaying was clearly of good quality and not ostentatious. Her clothes tended to emphasise, though not blatantly or with vulgarity, a build which was less than slender. However, its plumpness was firm and offered no suggestion of being comprised of over-indulgent fat. It was comprised of a large bosom, a reasonably trim waist and fully curvaceous hips of a kind held by the male population of the period to be the ideal female figure.

Watching the hostlers who were present starting to unload a fair amount of expensive baggage, implying the newcomer was intending to make an extended stay in the town, considerable speculation was aroused amongst the spectators. A variety of suggestions, some created more on wishful thinking rather than logic, and others based upon over imaginative, even romantic, reasoning were being produced—if not mentioned openly—to account for her arrival and apparent intention to remain in Tennyson.

One school of thought, predominantly masculine,

wondered if the blonde might perhaps be a rich widow from the East who had come to Texas in search of a more virile replacement husband than was available back home.

In a similar vein, drawing conclusions from her calm poise, assurance and excellent taste in clothing, some of the crowd concluded she could be a famous theatrical lady touring the Lone Star State to forget a love affair which had gone wrong. However, this did not explain why she was planning to stay in Tennyson. Despite its growth, the town boasted only one saloon of any size and, even when the owner was present, this rarely imported entertainers. It seemed highly unlikely that Maxwell Higgins would change his policy whilst absent on vacation.

By far the most imaginative line of reasoning decided the newcomer might have 'gone to Texas', to use a popular saying of the day, while on the run from the law after having been involved in some spectacular major crime—of passion, in all probability—wherever she had come from.

It must be confessed that the subscribers to this particular theory were in a minority!

Nor, although he was eyeing her with as much interest as the other spectators, was the elderly deputy marshal one of the few contemplating such a fanciful notion. He did, nevertheless, conclude his superior would be interested to hear of her arrival and any other information which might be forthcoming. She was, asserted his instincts acquired by many years of serving as a peace officer, no ordinary visitor or potential permanent resident.

If the blonde was aware of the speculation generated by her descent from the stagecoach, or noticed the scrutiny to which she was being subjected on all sides, she gave not the slightest indication of it. Instead, she accepted the bulky brown pigskin valise which the shotgun messenger had collected from inside the vehicle, and went to where the driver was talking with the agent for the Wells Fargo company.

'Good afternoon,' the woman greeted, as the driver took and started to sign the delivery receipt book with which he had been presented. Her voice had the friendly assurance of one long accustomed to associating with men on closer to equal terms than was usual in that day and age, but—except it did not suggest her origins were south of the Mason-Dixon line—her accent was undefinable as to a specific region. 'Can you fix it to have what I don't take along of my gear fetched down to the Hide And Horn for me, please?'

'Cert—!' the agent commenced automatically, being long accustomed to receiving such a request from incoming passengers. Then, as he heard the various excited comments which were rising from the crowd, a full appreciation of what had been asked of him struck home and he squawked rather than merely inquired, 'The *Hide And Horn?*'

'The *Hide And Horn,*' the blonde confirmed, placing a similar emphasis upon the name of the destination she had given, and still not taking the slightest notice of the response elicited by her words amongst the people standing around. 'You do know where it is, don't you?'

'Of course I know where it is, ma'am!' the agent declared, swinging his gaze involuntarily along Vernon Street in the direction of the establishment under discussion; although it could not be seen from where they were standing. 'B-But it's a *saloon!*'

'Well, yes,' the newcomer answered, with a suggestion of dry humour which nontheless avoided out and out sarcasm. 'That's what good old Maxie Higgins told me it was when he figured his king high flush had my eights and sevens full house licked.[3] So, seeing as how it didn't, I hope it's as good a *saloon* as he claimed it to be.'

3. *A detailed description of the relative value of the 'hands' in the game of poker is given in:* TWO MILES TO THE BORDER. *J.T.E.*

There was a calm confidence about the blonde as she was delivering the pronouncement, which implied she 'knew her way around'. It also suggested she was fully aware that the information she was imparting would be of considerable interest to more than just the man she was addressing, but that she was not unduly concerned over the type of public opinion which was starting to be expressed by one section of the crowd.

As was only to be expected, what the newcomer had said was meeting with a mixed reception!

However, only the majority of the men present were expressing various stages of approval. While the younger members of the Ladies Guild For Civic Betterment might consider her purpose in coming to Tennyson suggested a defiance of convention to be commended, they were too wise to publicly voice such a point of view. The remainder, a group of dried-up, vinegar-faced wives, spinsters and maiden aunts who were the power in the association, started shaking their heads, clucking their tongues and audibly mumbling their disapprobation.

'Disgusting!'

'Shocking!'

'This is a disgrace!'

'What will the new Governor say?'

'Marshal Collier must be told of this!'

Despite hearing various adverse comments, as it was intended she should, the blonde did not attempt to reply verbally. Instead, she turned and ran a glance around her critics. Something in her demeanour brought the cackle of remarks to a halt. Despite their usual assumption of superiority over everybody not fortunate enough to belong to their select circle, not one of the objectors was willing to match her gaze and all found something else to which to give their attention.

'Hey there, cowboy.' the newcomer exclaimed, concluding she could leave a confrontation with the "good" women of the community until later, and turning her eyes to the nearest of the masculine spectators. Gesturing with the pigskin valise grasped in her left hand, she went on, 'Happen you tote this along to the Hide And Horn *Saloon* for me, should you be able to get that far without needing to fork a horse, there'll be free drinks at the bar for you tonight.'

'Well now, ma'am,'' drawled the man to whom the request was made, deciding the blonde must be well acquainted with the ways of cowhands to have phrased it in such a fashion. 'I reckon, going deep and sore 'gainst the grain though it be, I can just about get that far a-foot when there's free drinks at the end of the trail. Is it just the one bag you want toting?'

'I reckon I can manage the reticule myself,' the blonde confirmed, nodding at the somewhat larger than usual piece of feminine accoutrement in her right hand, and then nodding to five larger portmanteaus which had been taken from the boot at the rear of the stagecoach by the hostlers. 'The rest can come down later. There isn't any all-fired rush, though, so long as I get them before we close up tonight.'

'I'll have them delivered as soon as the stage is gone, ma'am,' the agent promised, the last sentence having been directed at him. 'Will that be all right?'

'Any time that's convenient for you. If I'm not there, I'll have left word where I want them putting,' the woman replied amiably, then returned her attention to her assistant. 'We might as well head them up and move them out, friend.'

'I'll ride point for you, ma'am,' the cowhand offered, amused by the employment of the traditional command given by a trail boss to set a herd of half wild longhorn cattle into motion.

Despite the obvious disapproval of the Ladies Guild For Civic Betterment, belonging as he did to a section of the local population whose activities in town rarely met with their approbation, the cowhand showed no hesitation before accepting the item of baggage he was offered. He grunted as he felt its weight, which proved to be considerably greater than he had expected from the ease its owner had shown while handling it. Then, with the hostile glares of the 'good' women bouncing unheeded from their backs, he accompanied her along the street in the direction of the Hide And Horn Saloon. Her stride was confident as, avoiding the less than smooth planks of the sidewalk, she strolled leisurely and surveyed her surroundings. Yet, while her gait was undeniably feminine, it had none of the blatant hip-rolling and buttock swaying locomotion to which members of the Ladies Guild For Civic Betterment could have taken exception as befitting only a 'fallen' woman.

'Happen you don't reckon I'm being all nosey, ma'am,' the cowhand remarked, after a few seconds. 'But are you aiming to run the Hide And Horn all on your lonesome?'

'Shucks, no,' the woman replied. 'Should they be of a mind to stay on and we find we can get along, I aim to keep whoever Maxie Higgins had working for him to do the lifting and toting for me. There's no fun being a boss and doing all the work yourself. That's not what bosses are for.'

'Likely not,' the cowhand conceded, guessing the decision over whether the blonde and the members of the staff could 'get along' would be made by her rather than them. However, having developed a liking for her and considering she deserved something more than just the service he was rendering in return for the free drinks which would be forthcoming, he went on soberly, 'It's allus been a real tough place, ma'am.'

'Has, huh?'

'Yes'm. Word has it's how ole Maxie was finding it too much for him and's been looking for somebody to take it off his hands.'

'He found *me*,' the woman asserted, but without any display of concern over what she had heard. 'Only we didn't exactly sit head to head and do any horse-trading before it changed hands. He said, "I'll call", I

20

showed him my eights and sevens full and he handed over the title deeds like a gentleman.'

'Likely he was pleased to see it go,' the cowhand claimed.

'Maybe,' the blonde replied. 'But I've won her and, comes what may, I'm aiming to stay with her no matter how tough a place she might be.'

CHAPTER TWO

It Belongs To *Me* Now

While carrying on the conversation with the cow-hand, the buxom blonde had been studying what could be seen of Vernon Street, Tennyson's main thoroughfare. At first, due to the way this was laid out, the premises she had acquired were not in view. Nevertheless, she gave a nod expressing satisfaction with what she was able to see. Yet, to a casual observer, there did not appear to be any reason for her reaction.

The town did not seem to be any more impressive, or noticeably better favoured, than numerous other such small communities which dotted the vast open range country from the eastern boundary of Texas to the Pacific Ocean. Building materials might differ according to the climatic conditions and terrain of each specific region, ranging from stone and logs in the north to pure adobe or a mixture of adobe and wooden planks in the south. There would undoubtedly be different names on, or even varying designations given to, the same kind of business premises. However, the basic layout and services which were offered remained much the same, even if they were not found in identical locations.

Somewhere in the community there would probably be at least one bank, hotel, undertaker's parlour, doctor's surgery, gunsmith's and saddler's shops, general store—which frequently served as post office in smaller places—livery barn, saloon or similar place of entertainment, perhaps a brothel—albeit, discreetly situated beyond the view of the more respectable citizens' dwellings—offices for civic authorities and the local law enforcement agencies, the latter generally being accommodated in the jailhouse. There would also be places of worship available for those who followed certain religious creeds, but these were less often in evidence upon the main street which was generally given over to civic and commercial enterprises.

Having advanced sufficiently along Vernon Street, the woman turned her gaze to the frontage of the Hide And Horn Saloon. Two storeys high, it appeared to be a substantial structure. While in need of some painting, its wooden planks showed no sign of neglect nor unrepaired damage caused by exposure to the elements. A veranda with a chest high guard rail went all around the second floor, allowing the occupants of its rooms to step out and enjoy a breath of fresh air instead of having to walk downstairs and leave the premises.

On the ground floor, a set of double doors—closed at that moment—gave admittance to the bar-room. The big front windows were painted white over their lower halves, reducing the chance of minors becoming corrupted by watching their elders enjoying the various pleasures within. The big sign board attached to the guard rail of the veranda bore a somewhat garish illustration depicting a herd of longhorn cattle on the trail. As these half domesticated creatures had helped Texas to grow 'from hide and horn' out of the serious financial problems which had resulted from having supported the South in the War Between The States, this accounted for the name of the establishment.[1]

1. *How the exploitation of the longhorn cattle brought prosperity to Texas is told in:* GOODNIGHT'S DREAM, FROM HIDE AND HORN *and* SET TEXAS BACK ON HER FEET. *J.T.E.*

After having surveyed the exterior of the premises which she claimed to have won, the blonde examined its immediate surroundings. Considering the ambitions she had in mind for her acquisition, she decided these too met with her approval. In her experienced opinion, the saloon could hardly have been erected in a better location.

Either by accident or design, Vernon Street had been widened until it formed what the local people called the Square—despite it being closer to an oblong in shape. As the immediate neighbours to the left and right of the saloon were buildings which housed the County Land Agent and other civic offices, and the Cattleman's Bank, neither was likely to have residents upon the premises at night from whom there might be protests over being disturbed by sounds of revelry from the bar-room. Although the Fortescue Hotel was directly opposite, it was about a hundred yards away. Sufficiently far, in fact, to reduce the chances of complaints being made by the guests about the noise. Furthermore, providing her plans went as she envisaged, the blonde was confident good relations would ensue due to the owners benefitting from the quality of certain customers she was hoping to attract. There was no church near by, nor other buildings which gave indications of serving as places of worship for less established creeds (from whom exception might have been taken as to the pleasures she would be offering). At the north side on the eastern end of the Square was the jailhouse, serving as a repository for those who broke the law or merely disturbed the peace by having celebrated not wisely but too well.

'Who's the great seizer hereabouts, friend?' the woman inquired, after having concluded her scrutiny.

'The *what*, ma'am?' asked the cowhand.

'Come on now, you know who I mean,' the blonde stated with a grin. 'Or, happen you don't, being a right law-abiding gent, who's the lawman, constable, town

24

marshal, county sheriff, or whoever keeps house down to the pokey.'

'Lloyd Bowman's county sheriff, ma'am,' the cowhand replied, amused by how the question had finally been posed; although his tone indicated he did not hold the official about whom he was speaking in very high regard. 'Only he's down to Garnett, which being the county seat, most of the time we don't see much of him up here, nor want to. Tune Collier's town marshal. Happen you've heard of him?'

'I've heard something about him,' the woman admitted, despite sensing she had been expected to disclaim all knowledge.

'He's not so well known's some,' the cowhand asserted, deciding the blonde had spent more time around Texas than her accent suggested. 'As well as being marshal, he acts as deputy for Bowman, with ole Pockets Hoscroft backing his play.'

'And what do *you* reckon of Town Marshal-cum-Deputy Sheriff Tune Collier?' the woman asked, genuinely interested in receiving his opinion.

'He's as square's they come and they don't come no squarer,' the cowhand declared, in a tone far different from that he had used when speaking of the county sheriff. 'Treats *everybody* fair, which's more'n some do with us cow-nurses. And it's not just 'cause he's scared to do otherwise. Should the need come, he's tough enough.'

'Huh huh!' the woman grunted, her manner showing appreciation, despite the non-committal response. Then she gave a shrug and went on, 'Oh well, I reckon I'll soon enough be meeting him. First off, though, I conclude it's time for me to take a closer look at what I've won.'

Crossing the sidewalk along which she and her companions had been walking, the blonde gripped the knob of the closed front doors. On turning it, she discovered the main entrance was neither locked nor bolted. Pushing the door open, she stepped into the

25

main bar-room of the Hide And Horn Saloon. Having crossed the threshold, she paused and gazed about her with an even greater interest than she had shown while studying the outside of the building.

At first glance, a new owner—even one who had gained posession of the premises as a result of incautious betting on the part of the previous proprietor—might have found the view somewhat depressing!

There was not a single paying customer present!

On either side of the long mahogany counter, which the blonde noticed bore a gloss indicating it had recently been polished, two waiters and the only bartender on duty were idly matching throws with five dice from a glass tumbler instead of the more usually employed leather cup. A dozen female employees were present, but hardly occupied gainfully. Clad in brightly coloured dresses—which left arms, shoulders and the upper half of the bosom exposed to view—ending just below kneel level, they were sitting around one of the tables not equipped for gambling which was covered with the remains of the meal they had been eating.

The mirror behind the bar showed no reflection of business being done, but its surface had obviously been wiped recently to keep it clean. The same applied to the glasses which were waiting to be filled. However, despite the evidence of care having been lavished upon this most important area, only a few bottles of liquor stood on the capacious shelves. Elsewhere, the doors which gave access to the rooms at the rear and afforded exits at the sides of the building were all closed. Nobody was ascending the wide staircase, nor coming down from the indoor balcony and accomadation on the second floor.

To the left side of the bar-room, not far from a door upon which was inscribed in white paint, 'PRIVATE, Maxwell L. Higgins, Prop.', the faro layout had a green cloth covering its top which was traditionally decorated by a tiger. Elsewhere, the *vingt-un* and

26

chuck-a-luck outfits stood idle and unattended. Nor was the wheel-of-fortune on its stand against the right side wall being spun by an operator. In fact, nowhere was there any sign of whoever might be employed to handle the gambling portion of the business.

However, regardless of the dearth of activity and profitable business, the newcomer was not unduly depressed by what she saw. Posessing considerable experience where such matters were concerned, although this was the first time she had actually been the proprietor, she concluded things would soon liven up once news of her arrival and claim to ownership was spread. Unless she missed her guess, as soon as they had dealt with whatever business had taken them to the Wells Fargo depot—or learned such news as was brought by the driver and shotgun messenger, particularly with regards to the latest developoments at the State capital—a good proportion of the men who had witnessed her descent from the stagecoach would make for the saloon to see how she intended to run it and if she had been telling the truth about her status.

Furthermore, regardless of the lengthy absence of the previous owner, the blonde could detect no evidence of neglect. The fact that the stock behind the bar appeared to be less than was desirable did not strike her as being of any great importance. In fact, she considered anything which remained would be in the nature of a bonus for she had arranged for fresh supplies to arrive in the next day or so. With the exception of the table being used by the girls, everything was clean and tidy. This suggested the employees had been adequately supervised by the man left in charge by Maxwell Higgins.

Lounging at the 'sober' side of the counter, and announcing he had three kings to beat, the bartender glanced towards the front entrance as he realized somebody had entered. Tall, burly in a firm fleshed and solidly muscled way, he was in his mid-thirties. He had black hair parted down the middle, a luxuriant

27

moustache and a cheerful cast of features. Clad in a collarless light blue shirt, black trousers and Hersome gaiter boots, the white apron about his waist was clean. Surprised by what he saw, he performed what members of the theatrical profession called a 'double take' and hurriedly laid aside the glass. Noticing his reaction, his opponents and the girls were induced to follow the direction in which he was staring and they too gazed in puzzlement at the newcomer.

'Excuse me, ma'am,' said the taller of the waiters, clad—as was his companion—in much the same way as the bartender. Having recovered his wits before anybody else, he had drawn his own conclusions from the sight of the cowhand who was carrying a brown pigskin valise and standing just behind the blonde. Suspecting she was being subjected to the kind of practical joke for which members of that hard riding, hard working and harder playing fraternity were noted, he went on, 'I reckon you must've got brought to the wrong place. The hotel's across the Square out there. This is a *saloon*.'

'Well now,' the woman answered, starting to walk forward with purposeful strides. 'I hadn't got around to figuring it was anything other than a *saloon* and I for sure don't need to go to any hotel. Maxie Higgins told me he kept rooms set out as living quarters right here.'

'You *know* Maxie, ma'am?' the bartender inquired, his voice deep and having the accent of a Texan, as he threw an involuntary glance at the second floor balcony and then to one girl in particular at the table.

'We met up one night in the Silver Bell at Fort Worth is all,' the woman replied, halting and placing her reticule on the counter.

'Just the *one* night, ma'am?' queried the shorter and older waiter, jumping to conclusions and thinking this was a remarkably short acquaintance to have elicited an offer of accomodation.

'Just the one was enough,' the blonde declared, showing none of the resentment or annoyance which

28

the implication behind the question might have produced. 'And I surely hope he was better at running this place than he was at playing poker. Not that it matters how he used to run it, anyways.'

'Excuse me, ma'am,' the man behind the counter put in. Being a keen student of character, he concluded there was more, *much* more in fact, to the newcomer than appeared on the far from unimpressive surface. He also could not reconcile a person such as he suspected her to be, having formed the obvious kind of relationship with Maxwell Higgins. 'But did you say, "*used to run it*"?'

'That's what I said,' the blonde confirmed. 'And, no matter how he ran it, likely I won't be doing it that way.'

'How do you mean, ma'am?' the first waiter to speak inquired. 'You won't be doing it that way.'

'It means just like it sounds,' the woman stated, aware that everybody present was paying great attention to what she was saying. 'Seeing as how it belongs to *me* now, I'll be running this place from today.'

'It belongs to *you*?' queried the shorter waiter, throwing a glance at the bartender. 'Hot damn, ma'am, do you mean Maxie don't own it any more?'

'That's just what I mean, nothing more and nothing less,' the blonde confirmed. 'Any time a feller bets his saloon on a flush against somebody who's holding a full house, you can lay all you've got that it's going to change hands as soon as he calls.'

'Maxie did that again' *you*, ma'am?' asked the man behind the counter, remembering something he had heard about the establishment at which the newcomer claimed to have made the acquaintance of Higgins.

'Sounds almost like you reckon he was way too slick a poker player to do it, friend,' the woman said dryly, but without animosity, waving her gloved left hand towards the reticule. 'Anyways, I'm not asking you to take nothing more than just my word on it and wouldn't be expecting you to. I've got the deeds to the place in here, signed over to me all neat and legal, along with letters explaining things for Counselor Aloysius P. Scrope, attorney at law, and Joe Turner—!'

'That's me, ma'am,' the bartender admitted, the explanation having been brought to an end and an interrogatory glance directed his way.[2]

'Somehow, I thought it just might be,' the woman conceded, her tone amiable. 'Maxie spoke highly of you, Joe. Now, afore I do anything else, I want you to come with me to Counselor Scrope's office. That way I'll be able to prove I'm telling the truth to both of you at the same time.'

'Sure thing, ma'am,' Turner assented without hesitation, already convinced the change of ownership had taken place as described. Although at best an indifferent player, Maxwell Higgins had never let this deter him from joining games of poker for high stakes and there was one such game in particular held regularly at the Silver Bell Saloon in Fort Worth which often saw considerable sums of money and even property change hands. 'I'll take you there right now, but——!'

The bartender was not allowed to finish!

At their table, the saloongirls had been watching and listening to everything that was said. Such had been their interest, the rest had stopped paying even token attention to the story being told by one of their number concerning the part she had played in a certain well known bar-room fracas. Having studied the newcomer throughout the conversation, they then turned their gaze back to the story teller in a manner redolent of expectancy mingled with challenge. Know-

2. *Due to what we suspect—for reasons we explain at the conclusion of,* CUT ONE, THEY ALL BLEED—*was a deliberate error in the source from which we produced,* 'Better Than Calamity', *we attributed ownership of the 'Bull's Head Saloon', as we had been led to assume it was called, to Joseph Turner. The additional information with which we have now been supplied has allowed us to make the appropriate corrections. J.T.E.*

ing what was expected of her by her female associates and having another reason much stronger than a mere desire to retain their esteem, she shoved back her chair. Coming to her feet, she stalked with an arrogant and hip rolling motion towards the woman who claimed to have supplanted the previous owner.

Suddenly, the atmosphere became charged with tension!

The employees of the saloon and the cowhand, who had followed the blonde and placed the valise alongside her at the bar, knew Viola Grant to be a tough proposition. Tall, brunette, good looking and shapely in a Junoesque fashion, she was regarded as the boss girl by virtue of her ability in a hair-yanking brawl and also for having been on *very* close terms with the man who, according to the newcomer, was no longer the proprietor of the establishment.

'So you're the new *boss*, huh?' the brunette demanded, rather than inquired, ignoring the prohibitive glare she recieved from Turner and planting herself directly in front of the blonde on spread apart legs and with arms akimbo.

'Well, yes,' the newcomer answered, turning and allowing the reticule she had retrieved to slip back on to the counter. She had been keeping the reactions of the saloongirls under observation via the reflection in the mirror behind the bar and now ran her gaze over what she knew represented the first challenge to her authority. 'Comes right down to it, I'll have to admit all modest and humble that I'm the new *boss*.'

'I was in the Battle At Bearcat Annie's,' Viola announced, wondering if the buxom woman had heard of the event she had been describing to her companions.[3]

'On whose side?' the blonde inquired, sounding almost meek.

'Bearcat's, of course!'

3. *A description of the 'Battle At Bearcat Annie's, is given in:* QUIET TOWN. *J.T.E.*

'That's *interesting*, but what does it have to do with *me*?'

'Just this!' Viola stated. 'After what I done there, I don't take kind' to the notion of a *woman* figuring on giving me *orders*.'

'There's *some* might say that's reasonable,' the blonde declared, sounding as if considering she was conferring a favour. 'But it all depends on what you *did* there.'

'I was in the thick of the fighting!' the brunette announced.

'Is that *all*?' the newcomer sniffed, showing no indication of being impressed. 'Way I heard it, Bearcat Annie and all her girls got whupped real good that night, in spite of the odds being long in their favour.'

'I got put out by accident afore it was half over!' Viola claimed, hearing sniggers from the table she had left and supplying her usual excuse with an air of considering this alone explained the adverse result. 'And that's the only god-damned time anything like it's happened to me!'

'Do tell?' the blonde said, but there was no longer any suggestion of meekness about her. 'Now me, I've always believed there's a *second* time for *everything*!'

'Is that what you *believe*, huh?' the brunette asked, conscious of her reputation for 'taking no sass but sarsparila' being at stake. She was also aware that the favours she had received due to her association with Higgins were threatened. The thought had opened up another line of speculation. Although he had promised to do so, he had not sent for her to join him wherever he had selected to spend his vacation. She wondered if he had contracted a similar alliance with the newcomer, who was sent—pretending to have won the saloon—to either remove her forcibly, or offer an excuse for him to fire her on his return. 'Well this ain't the "mother-something" day for it to happen!'[4]

4. *See the third paragraph of our* Author's Note. *J.T.E.*

CHAPTER THREE

Call Me 'Madam Bulldog'

Having delivered the pronouncement, Viola Grant swung her right hand in what was intended to be a hard slap to the face of the buxom blonde newcomer. It was a method of attack which had served her well in the past. Submitted as suddenly and—as she believed it would be at that moment—unexpectedly, similar tactics had invariably reduced whatever resistance the recipient might have been contemplating. Or, if reprisals were attempted, their effect was lessened due to the tears of pain caused by the force of the blow.

However, to achieve the desired results, the slap first had to land!

Instead of being caught unawares by the attack, the blonde responded to it with speed and competence!

Throwing up her left arm, the newcomer deftly blocked and deflected the approaching hand before it even came close to making contact with her cheek. Having done so, she knotted her right hand into a fist. The way she brought this around indicated she was well versed in such matters. Dropping her right shoulder to put all the weight of her curvaceous and clearly powerful stocky body into the effort, she smashed her knuckles and not the flat of the palm with the force of a mule's kick to the side of the brunette's unguarded jaw.

Caught as solidly and even harder than she had

anticipated her intended victim would be, Viola was twirled on her heels then returned at a headlong rush in the direction from which she had come. Seeing her approaching, clearly without exercising any control over her movements, the other saloongirls gave vent to squeals of surprise and alarm while starting to hurriedly rise. Nor was the latter precaution unjustified. Spinning back, the brunette collided and fell across the table. Despite its width, and her weight combined with the momentum of her arrival, caused it to turn over sideways. Accompanied by the plates, cups, saucers, silverware, cruet, a jug of milk, bowl of sugar and coffeepot—the last three all but empty as luck would have it—she was deposited on the floor. Rolling over, until flat on her back, she sprawled supine and motionless.

As became one who had spent many years in his present line of work, Joseph Turner felt he could claim to be something of a connoisseur where fisticuffs—whether in a formal 'prize' ring, or a roughhouse brawl—were concerned. He concluded that the right cross thrown by the woman, who he did not doubt was to be his new employer, had been delivered as competently as any he had ever witnessed. Furthermore, in his considered opinion, it had been performed deliberately and with a skill which could be repeated, rather than merely being the result of chance. It was, in fact, the kind of a blow which could end a fight without the need for repetition.

Knowing from past experience how well Viola could handle herself in physical combat, the girls who had quit the table were equally impressed by what had happened. While willing to concede over-confidence had been a contributory factor to her downfall, none of them believed luck was in any way responsible for the punch which had returned her to them in such a precipitous fashion.

Therefore, with the exception of a buxom red head and a more slender 'blonde'—whose hirsute coloura-

tion was so obviously produced by artificial aids it had
earned her the sobriquet, 'Bottles'—the girls were
content to accept they had a new employer to be
respected. Being particular cronies of the recumbent
brunette, the exceptions had had a few privileges as a
result of their connection with her. In addition to
feeling a certain loyalty, although they did not doubt
the blonde was telling the truth when explaining what
had brought her to the Hide And Horn Saloon, they
were just as sure of what would befall them should
Viola learn, on regaining consciousness, that they had
let the attack go unavenged. With that in mind, they
darted towards the bar.

Seeing the pair heading her way, the newcomer
guessed their motives with some accuracy and formed
a shrewd assessment of their respective abilities. She
concluded that neither was as formidable an antago-
nist as the brunette would have been. Therefore, she
was not perturbed nor unduly worried by their obviously hostile intentions. She had felt sure, even before
her arrival, that her authority would be challenged by
the female members of the staff and was not averse to
being presented with such an early opportunity to
demonstrate her willingness and skill to cope with
matters of that nature.

'Stop anybody coming in, boys!' the blonde commanded, having heard enough to suggest there was a
possibility of customers arriving, directing the words
to the two waiters.

Having darted glances at the bartender and receiving a nod of confirmation, the two men hurried across
to the front entrance. They arrived just in time to
prevent the first of the spectators from the Wells Fargo
depot coming in. Having closed and locked the doors,
they turned to watch what was taking place. They
found, short as the time taken had been, that their new
employer appeared to have the situation well in hand.

Without having waited to find out whether her
instructions would be carried out, the newcomer had

35

stepped to meet her two would-be assailants. Having had somewhat the shorter distance to cover and being in the lead, the red head was subjected to her attentions first. Bringing up and spreading apart both arms, to push aside the hands reaching for her hair, she placed her flat right palm against the other's face. Twisting her torso slightly to offer an added force, she gave a shove. Finding her advance turned into an even more hurried retreat, the red head did not stop until tripping over and landing upon her rump beyond the recumbent and unprotesting Viola.

Having disposed of the first intended avenger, the blonde devoted her next efforts to the second. Startled by the ease with which Sally had been removed, Bottles tried to bring to a stop what she now realized to be an incautious and potentially dangerous approach. Although she started to lower the hands raised ready to grab the newcomer, her change of intentions proved of no avail. The buxom woman was already launching a backhand slap which landed and sent her reeling after the red head. A wail of mortification and pain burst from her as she collapsed on top of Sally. However, neither was rendered *hors de combat* and the mocking laughter of the other girls goaded each into a desire to repay the rough treatment to which they had been subjected. Spluttering profanities, they rolled apart and into kneeling postures from which they meant to rise and resume the attack in a more concerted fashion.

Showing that she was aware they might not intend to allow the affair to come to a peaceful end, the blonde strode after Bottles as she was following Sally. Grasping each by the scruff of the neck, she jerked them from their hands and knees until almost erect. Granting them not the slightest opportunity to resist and showing no sign of being inconvenienced by supporting their combined weights, she brought their foreheads together in a snapping motion. Stunned by the collision, they went limp and she pushed so they fell across the unmoving body of their friend.

'Any more of you ladies figuring on getting in on the dance?' the blonde asked, swinging a glance to each of the remaining saloongirls in turn. When there was no suggestion of an acceptance to what had clearly been a challenge, she looked at the bartender and went on, 'Do you have a bucket of water back there, Joe?'

'Yes, ma'am,' Turner replied, showing admiration.

'Let me have it, please,' the woman requested, working the fingers of her right hand. 'And you don't need to keep saying, "ma'am". I wasn't given time to say so before, but you can call me "Madam Bulldog".'

'Yes, ma—Madam Bulldog!' the bartender assented.

Trying to remember what it was about the name he found vaguely familiar, Turner bent and picked up the sizeable oaken bucket filled with water; which was to have been used for washing glasses when the business of the day was commenced. He placed it on the counter, meaning to go around and carry out whatever further instructions he might be given. The need to do so did not arise. Strolling over and picking it up, regardless of its weight, the blonde carried it with only one hand as she returned to where her three victims were beginning to stir. Gripping the bottom with her other hand, she upended it to pour the contents over them. To the accompaniment of gasps, which turned into wails and spluttering squeals, they were brought back to full consciousness. Struggling apart, they sat in slumped and bedraggled discomfiture looking worriedly at the cause of their misfortunes.

'You likely didn't hear me just now,' the blonde said, tossing aside the bucket and standing, with hands on hips, just beyond the reach of any of the trio who should show an inclination to resume hostilities. 'What I said was, the name's "Madam Bulldog". I'm your new *boss*—Any *objections*?'

For a moment, although she was sufficiently recovered to hear and understand what had been said,

Viola did not answer. Nor, satisfied to follow her lead, did either of her would-be avengers offer to comment. Sniffing in pain, the brunette reached with a hand to gingerly move her jaw and which felt twice its normal size. However, even though she doubted whether she would feel capable of eating steak for a while, she concluded it was not broken. Staring upwards through the involuntary tears and water dribbling from her soaked hair, she reached a rapid decision. Even if she was correct in her assumption over the real reason for the arrival of the blonde, the acceptance of the story shown by Joe Turner notwithstanding, she considered it was advisable to 'holler calf rope'—as cowhands put it—and surrender. Unless she was mistaken, Madam Bulldog stood ready, willing and more than able to wade in tooth and claw, or with hard fists more likely, to quell any further objections. After having received one sample, for all her personal toughness, Viola wanted no more.

'N—No, *boss!*' the brunette declared with a vehemence which caused suffering to her swollen jaw.

'How about you two?' the blonde inquired.

'N—Not me, *boss!*' Bottles and Sally asserted in practically the same breath and fashion, each being equally disinclined to render assistance even if their friend decided to take up the challenge.

'Then that's an *end* to it!' Madam Bulldog stated, her manner implying it would go hard with anybody who did not accept her ruling on the issue. 'You'd all best go get into some dry clothes and red up again before we let the paying customers in.'

Watching the trio help one another to rise and practically scuttle off to obey her orders, the blonde became aware that somebody was being granted admission in spite of her instructions. Swinging around quickly, with the intention of establishing straight away that she expected all her orders to be carried out by male as well as female employees, she raised no objections on seeing who it was. While it was permissible for her to deny access to members of the public at her convenience, applying such a restriction to local peace officers—particularly on the day of her arrival—would be far from diplomatic even if to do so without a good reason was possible.

'Howdy, marshal,' Madam greeted amiably, having made the deduction from the shape of the badge of office for one thing. Walking forward and nodding to the second of the men who had been allowed to enter, she went on, 'I saw your deputy there looking me over down to the Wells Fargo depot, then light a shuck like the Devil caught in a holy water throwing. So I figured it wouldn't be long before you dropped by. Does *all* your family run so much to height and heft?'

There was justification in the latter comment!

Over six foot tall, Town Marshal Tune Collier was a well set up figure of a man. Nor had forty-five years of life in Texas, twenty-four of which had been spent serving as a peace officer in various places, brought more than just a tinge of grey to the temples of his brown hair. There was a suggestion of a lively sense of humour about his clean shaven, tanned and ruggedly handsome features and his clothing was of a quality which implied he was sufficiently honest to be living on his salary, instead of supplementing it by dubious, or downright illicit, means. He was wearing a low crowned, wide brimmed tan J.B. Stetson hat, an unfastened and loose fitting brown jacket over an open necked grey shirt, a tightly rolled dark blue bandana knotted around his throat, yellowish brown Nankeen trousers and low heeled, polished black riding boots. The brown gunbelt around a waist which was more slender than the spread to his shoulders, albeit not quite so much as formerly, carried a rosewood handled Remington New Army Model of 1863 revolver at the left side in a cross draw holster. Having clearly seen considerable use, rig and weapon were well maintained.

'I hail from the itty-bitty side of it, ma'am,' the

marshal replied, his voice a pleasant drawl indicative of an upbringing in the Lone Star State. 'Have you run across many of us?'

'I can only claim a talking acquaintance with Big Ranse Counter and to having heard more than a mite about that boy of his, Mark,' Madam admitted. 'Big Ranse's nice people, but no poker player, even though he thinks real powerful he is.'

'Sounds like you know Cousin Ranse real good at that,' Collier declared, suspecting the blonde was aware her latter statement was incorrect and born out of a genuine liking for his kinsman which did not stem from the ownership of one of the largest ranches in the Big Bend country. Nor was he surprised that she had heard of 'that boy of his', Mark Counter having achieved considerable prominence since the end of the War Between The States.[1] Looking pointedly across the room, his voice took on a more official timbre as he continued, 'Mind if I ask what's been coming off here?'

'I've just been getting acquainted with the girls and making sure we're going to see eye to eye on me being the one who's running things,' Madam explained, also glancing to where the dishevelled and wet trio had halted and were watching. 'Now Joe Turner's going to take me to meet Counselor Scrope. Maybe you'd like to come along with us and see that I really do own the Hide And Horn?'

* * *

'Yes, these documents are genuine,' Aloysius P. Scrope reported, in his dry-as-dust Philadelphia accent. Tall, lean, with a sharp face having the texture of ancient parchment, his sombre clothes and manner gave no indication of the hearty and excellent company he could be on suitable occasions outside his

1. *Information regarding Mark Counter is given in the* Floating Outfit *series. J.T.E.*

office. 'And they definitely establish that you are the legal owner of the Hide And Horn Saloon, Mrs. Can—!'

'*Madam Bulldog*,' the buxom blonde interrupted, from where she was sitting between Tune Collier and Joseph Turner facing the attorney across his desk. 'That's the *only* name I want to be known by and, so far as I know, there's no law against it.'

'There is not,' Scrope confirmed. 'Unless it is for illicit purposes, the use of an alias is entirely permissible under the law.'

'And there's *nothing* to stop me running the Hide And Horn, I mean like it was a rooming house, or a women's clothes store?'

'Nothing at all. I know of no statute, whether at Federal, State, or county level, prohibiting a woman from owning and, indeed, personally running a saloon. Nor is there any municipal ordinance to that effect.'

'If there is, I've never come across it,' Collier asserted, the attorney having directed the last part of the statement chiefly his way. 'Which I've read them *all* from bellow to tail tip. As long as you run a straight place, you won't hear any complaints as far as I'm concerned.'

'You mean there's not got to be any watering down of the liquor, rolling fellers after they've been got liquored up, rigging all of the gambling so the house can't lose, nor running the old badger game?'[2] Madam inquired. 'Damn it, and there I was counting on doing all of them to help me turn a profit.'

'You would be *most* ill-advised to do so,' the lawyer warned, so seriously he might have believed all the illicit measures were to have been employed. 'And that is my opinion as your attorney, Madam Bulldog.'

---

2. *One version of this notorious confidence trick is described in:* Part Four, 'Another Type Of Badger Game', WANTED! BELLE STARR. *J.T.E.*

'Then, hot damn, I'll take it even if it means I go broke before I can pay your fee,' the blonde promised, with a similar air of seriousness. It became more genuine as she continued, 'And you can *count* on that, Marshal Collier.'

'I reckon I can, Madam,' the peace officer replied. 'Which being, you won't see hide nor hair of me.'

'Only in your *official* capacity, I hope,' the woman answered. 'Happen you play the same brand of poker as Big Ranse, I'll be right obliged to have you sit in against me. That should keep me from a pauper's grave.'

'I can't sit in on the same brand of poker as Cousin Ranse on a marshal's pay,' Collier warned. 'It doesn't come close to as high as he makes out from running the R Over C spread.'

'Way he plays poker, he has to make out high from running it,' Madam maligned and, although she was aware that such a reference to the small size of his pay from some peace officers would have been a hint for it to be supplemented by her, she felt sure this was not the marshal's intention. Turning her attention to the lawyer, she went on, 'One thing, Counsellor. Can I count on you to make sure there're no sneaky legal shenanigans to get a new civic ordinance slipped in to stop me before I can prove I'm not aiming to turn Tennyson into another Sodom and Gomorrah?'

'I think you can rely upon me for that,' Scrope claimed.

'And I'll be backing you up to the Green River on it,' Collier promised, his instincts as a peace officer suggesting the change of ownership could be of benefit to the town generally as well as the saloon. 'But, the way things are, there'll be some who'll take more than just a mite of convincing you don't aim to.'

'You mean with folks wanting so bad to get Tennyson made county seat?' Madam guessed, having been told of the controversy by the driver of the stagecoach while waiting for the team to be changed at a way station.

'That, and with the changes's are coming along down to Austin,' the peace officer agreed, impressed by the extent of the blonde's knowledge concerning local affairs. He was not allowed to raise another matter to do with the running of the saloon as at that point he was interrupted.

'Excuse me, father,' said the pretty daughter of the attorney, who served as his clerk. 'Mr. and Mrs. Ratchet have arrived for their appointment.'

'Very well,' Scrope replied. 'Tell them I'll see them as soon as I'm through with this lady.'

'Is there much more to talk about?' the marshal asked, knowing the couple to be very strait-laced and believing they would not be made to feel any better disposed to the new owner of the saloon if delayed on her behalf in keeping their appointment. 'I've got things waiting down to the jailhouse and I reckon Madam's wanting to get back and see what's doing in her place.'

'You should have been a diplomat, Tune,' the lawyer declared, having drawn a similar conclusion despite the instructions he had given. 'And, unless there is anything further you feel we must discuss *right now*, Madam, I think you can leave everything in my hands.'

'There's nothing that can't wait until tomorrow at least,' the blonde admitted, guessing why the suggestions to end the meeting had been made and concluding she had acquired two staunch friends. Noticing the girl had not left the room, she pushed back her chair and rose, commenting, 'Come on, Joe. It's time we were getting back so I can meet up with the rest of the crew.'

Watching Madam leaving, followed by Collier and Turner, the attorney frowned. While aware that the conclusion of their meeting had been a tactful act, he wished he had been able to raise the matter of the gambling at the saloon as this could prove to be a matter of grave concern for her.

CHAPTER FOUR

Maxie Didn't Hire Them

'Well now,' Madam Bulldog greeted, turning from the safe into which she had placed the brown pigskin valise—which she had taken with her when visiting Counselor Aloysius P. Scrope—and looking at half a dozen of her employees brought into the private office by Joseph Turner. 'I reckon you might all have a pretty fair notion why I've had you fetched in here.'

While going to see the lawyer, Turner had found his respect and liking for his new employer continuing to grow. On emerging from the saloon onto the sidewalk, upon which a fair sized crowd of men had gathered, watching with unconcealed expectation, she had told him to leave the front doors open. Although this had implied the Hide And Horn Saloon was now open for business, albeit under new ownership, she had not made any announcement to that effect. Nor had she paid any discernible attention to those members of the Ladies Guild For Civic Betterment who were hovering in the vicinity.

Seeing the buxom blonde was accompanied by the local peace officers and the bartender, who was carrying the pigskin valise, the 'good' women had speculated audibly that she was either being taken to the jailhouse for trying to obtain the saloon under false pretences, or was to be sent on her way in the stagecoach which had not yet departed. From the direction she and her party had taken, with the exception of Deputy Town Marshal Herman 'Pockets' Hoscroft—who had left to go about his duties—they had realized neither assumption was correct. However, according to snatches of conversation made just loudly enough to be overheard by her, the general concensus of their revised opinion was that one or the other would take place after Town Marshal Tune Collier had seen her claims proven invalid by the attorney on subjecting her to an investigation.

Annoyed by the behaviour of the women, Turner had decided they had met their match in Madam Bulldog. A less experienced and self confident person might have fallen into the error of openly flaunting her immunity from either of their expectations and further antagonizing them. She had avoiding doing anything of the sort. In fact, her demeanour had suggested she was merely attending to a piece of trivial, yet necessary, business before getting on with more important matters.

Returning to the saloon, Madam had discovered trade had become brisk in her absence. Although none of the gambling games were being operated, there were now several customers present who had not been in the crowd from the Wells Fargo depot. Authorizing a 'drink on the house', she had taken the valise from Turner and, politely declining offers to join various groups wishing to become better acquainted, had taken it into the office. While waiting for the bartender to carry out the instructions he had received before accompanying her to visit the lawyer, she had opened the safe with a key supplied by Maxwell Higgins and made enough room inside to insert what was a most valuable piece of her property. Noticing a couple of surprising omissions from the people she had requested to be brought to meet her, she had decided against asking why this was so and addressed those who were present.

'It could be to tell us how you're figuring on

doubling our pay, ma'am,' suggested the taller of the waiters who had been in the bar-room when the blonde had put in her first appearance. He was grinning broadly.

'Well, yes, it *could* be for that,' Madam replied, also smiling, as she returned to sit at the desk in the centre of the room. 'Only, before any of you start to figuring out how you're going to spend all that extra money, I'd best come right out and say it isn't.'

'Somehow I didn't reckon it would be,' the waiter admitted cheerfully.

'Now me,' went on a short and jovial man who had been serving behind the bar when summoned by Turner. 'I just hope it's not to tell us's you'll be paying us any *less*.'

'I'd say I'm going to pay you what you're *worth*,' the blonde asserted, running her gaze around the half circle of faces on the other side of the desk. They were studying her speculatively in return, but without hostility, and the comment from the jovial bartender had not held the timbre of an implied threat. 'But, if I do, I just *know* somebody's going to tell me you'll be damned if you'll work for that *little*.'

'Dad-blast and consarn it, ma'am!' protested the smaller of the two elderly men employed as swampers; to sweep floors, clean spittoons and perform other menial duties. 'How'd you know that was pre-zactly what I was going to say?'

'I just took one look and natural' thought *you* might,' the blonde claimed, but her manner was friendly. 'In fact, was I asked, I'd reckon you was there the *first* time it was said.'

'Well, no, ma'am,' the swamper contradicted, showing no offense, regardless of the implication that he was extremely old. 'I ain't *quite* that all fired ancient. But I do recollect my ole pappy telling momma on the night's they got hitched 's how he'd just heard good ole Georgie Washington say it when asked to be first President of these United States of America.'

46

Listening to the chuckles and watching the reaction to the brief exchange, Madam concluded it was being enjoyed. Nevertheless, while she knew she had been accepted by Turner, she realized that the others were reserving their judgement upon her. Nor did she underestimate how important it was for this to be favourable. Each was a leader in his, or her, special field and, as the blonde knew, it would be extremely difficult to run the saloon without their full support. Certainly it could not be done as she intended unless she was given their wholehearted co-operation. Therefore, it was essential to either win them over, or decide whether to even let them remain as employees. For this reason, she had not asked Turner to supply information about any of them. She preferred to make her own estimation of their respective worth without being influenced by preconceived ideas.

'You're boss girl, huh?' the blonde asked, turning her attention to Viola Grant.

'I used to be,' the brunette admitted.

'You still are, happen you want it and don't try to be boss over *me*,' Madam offered. 'I don't know what kind of deal you had with Maxie Higgins, nor want to. With me, you'll get ten dollars a month more than the other girls. For that, I'll expect you to keep them in line and make sure there's no trouble of any kind from them inside, or *outside*. Can you handle it?'

'I'll give it a damned good try, *boss*,' Viola assured, having received far better treatment than she had expected. At best, if she was not fired, she had believed she would lose the authority granted by her toughness and association with the previous owner. Instead, she had had her position confirmed and was granted an increase to her pay. She realized this had not been done out of a frightened desire to curry her favour and knew the privilege would have to be earned. 'There's one thing, though—!'

'What is it?'

47

'I've been living in Max—*Mr. Higgins'* rooms upstairs while he was away—!'

'Then I hope you're a whole heap tidier than I am,' Madam commented, but refrained from expressing her supposition that the occupancy had been of a longer duration.

'That's what I meant to tell you, boss,' the brunette confessed, looking uncomfortable. 'I'm not——!'

'So the rooms are a touch messed up?' the blonde guessed, as the words once more trailed to an inconclusive end.

'More'n just a *touch*,' Viola corrected, with an air of shame which came as a surprise to the men.

'Those two buddies of yours are quick to help you, aren't they?' Madam asked.

'Sally 'n' Bottles?'

'Nobody got around to introducing us all formal and proper, but I reckon that's who they must be.'

'We've worked places together for years,' Viola explained. 'That's why they tried to jump you.'

'And there I was thinking it could have been because our dresses *clashed*,' Madam declared with a smile. 'Anyways, I reckon they *might* be ready to start helping you again. My maid went down with the grippe and won't be along for a spell, so I'll be calling for *three* volunteers to make the rooms ready for me.'

'We'll get on it straight away, boss!' the brunette promised.

'It can wait until after you've heard what I'm going to say,' the blonde declared, her manner showing she considered the matter was closed. 'This is the way I'm going to have things r——!'

Before the instructions could be passed on, the door giving access to the side alley was unlocked from outside and thrown open to allow a man to stalk in!

An inch taller than Turner and several pounds heavier, the face of the intruder was surly and unshaven. No matter what the original colour of his hair might have been, it was turned black by an over liberal application of some sickly smelling lotion. While his loud pin striped suit had cost more than the clothing worn by any of the male employees, it was rumpled, stained and strained at the seams. Nor were his collarless light green shirt and Hersome gaiter boots any cleaner. Despite his truculent air, he was not wearing any kind of weapon in plain view.

'What's all this I've heard about Maxie selling out?' the newcomer challenged, slamming the door behind him and standing with his back to it.

'And who might *you* be?' Madam demanded, without answering the question.

'The name's Moses Stern,' the man introduced, his manner suggesting no more need be said upon the subject.

'Do you work here?' the blonde asked quietly, remaining seated at the desk.

'Do I *work* here?' Stern rumbled, swinging his gaze around the other employees. 'I'm head bouncer is all!'

'Head bouncer, huh?' Madam said, keeping her voice quiet, having been wondering why Turner had not brought one of that particular branch of the staff to meet her.

'That's who I am!' the newcomer confirmed, slapping both hands against a bulging and far from solid paunch. 'And I'm here to be showed something's *proves* you got this place from my brother-in-law the way you reckon you did, 'cause I don't believe a "mother-something" word of it and ain't figuring on letting you just walk in 'n' take over!'

Glancing around, Madam found all the other occupants of the office were watching her in a speculative fashion. Much to her satisfaction, she sensed the men in particular were awaiting her instructions. However, she knew the less than polite demand to produce proof of ownership constituted a threat to her authority which she must meet unaided. By doing so, if she could, she would strengthen the respect she felt sure was building. This in turn would ensure they would help her enforce her intentions for the way the saloon was to be operated. Nevertheless, she appreciated any action she attempted was fraught with danger. Certainly, considering the way she was asked, merely displaying the documents she had produced at the lawyer's office would not serve her purpose in this instance.

Sharing the latter summation formed by the blonde, Turner was alternating worried glances between her and the head bouncer. Knowing Stern to be reasonably competent at such work, the liking he had developed for his new employer notwithstanding, he realized there was nothing he could do to help her at that moment. She must be allowed to cope with the situation unaided.

'Well?' Stern demanded, taking the pause without response from the woman to indicate he was correct in his assumption regarding the change of ownership. 'Why don't you out 'n' show me something, you goddamned tail-peddler?'

'All I'll show you is the door you came through!' Madam stated, looking into the bleary and bloodshot eyes of the newcomer. Rotating the swivel chair slowly, until her legs were no longer in the space beneath the desk, she went on, 'You're not *my* brother-in-law, for which I thank the Good Lord, so I don't have to keep you on!'

'Is that so?' Stern spat out, dropping the key with which he had gained admittance and starting to lumber forward. 'We'll soon see happen I can make you change your mi—!'

Before the man could take his fourth step, or complete the threat, the blonde was thrusting herself from the chair. Showing an even greater speed than when dealing with the three saloongirls, she hurtled to meet him. Bending at the waist, she twisted and rammed her left shoulder into his chest. Such was the force with which he was struck, aided by the not inconsiderable weight of her shapely body, he was flung away from her. Crashing backwards against the wall, he was unable to prevent himself rebounding from it. While his wits were never quick to respond to the unexpected, he reached the unpleasant conclusion that his misfortunes might not yet be at an end.

The assumption proved painfully correct!

Having gained an advantage from her unanticipated reaction to the threatening behaviour, which she suspected was all the man had believed would be necessary to achieve his ends, the blonde had no intention of losing it. Despite the success she had attained, offering him an opportunity to recover could prove a costly mistake. Even though not in the peak of condition, he was larger and undoubtedly stronger than her. What was more, his duties had probably required him to deal with rambunctious or even violent customers on occasion and he must have more than a rudimentary knowledge of roughhouse self defense.

Stepping to meet Stern, whose arms were waving wildly in an attempt to regain some control over his movements, Madam gave the impression that she was intending to rake at his face with her left fingernails. Acting instinctively, without pausing to consider she was wearing gloves and could not employ such a feminine tactic, he started to tilt his head to the rear. Doing so caused his torso to advance. Bringing around her clenched right fist, instead of continuing the innocuous movement with the other hand, she stepped in to increase its power and buried it almost wrist deep into his unwisely offered stomach. Nobody who ate and drank to excess as he did, along with avoiding the effort required to keep in condition, could take a blow in such a vulnerable region without showing an adverse effect. What breath remained in his lungs was expelled in a 'whoosh' and he sat down to the accompaniment of a soggy thud. Letting out a wheeze that was intended to be a profane description of his attacker, he clawed under the left side of his coat with his right hand.

'Watch him, boss!' Viola yelled, having no liking for the head bouncer. It was he who had told the wife of Maxwell Higgins of their intimate relationship and this in turn had caused her to be left behind when the trip was commenced which resulted in the saloon changing hands. 'He's got a stingy gun under there!'

While grateful for the warning, considering it evidence of having acquired a loyal supporter on the distaff side of her employees, Madam had not required it. Keen eyed and knowledgeable, she had noticed the slight bulge caused by the concealed weapon and was already setting about protecting herself when the brunette spoke.

Reaching with both hands, the blonde grasped Stern by the shoulders and hauled him from the sitting posture. Amazed by the strength she was exhibiting, he allowed the Remington Double Deringer to remain in its place of concealment. Brought to his feet, he staggered on being released. Again the fist was propelled into his stomach. Folding over, he collapsed on to his knees and started to vomit. Then he dropped face forward on to the mess he was making. His body twitched and writhed spasmodically, but not in an attempt to rise and move to a cleaner spot.

'Is he really Maxie's brother-in-law?' the blonde inquired, turning as soon as her victim went limp and lay motionless at her feet.

'That's the only reason he got kept on as head bouncer,' Turner replied. 'He didn't show up half the time, but Maxie's missus wouldn't let him be fired.'

'Get him out of here!' the blonde commanded, nodding to indicate she had suspected what she was told.

'Yes'm!' the bartender assented cheerfully.

'And when he can take notice,' Madam continued, before the order be acted upon. 'Tell him to come and let *me* know, happen he still reckons I can't fire him.'

52

'It'll be a *pleasure*, boss,' Turner declared. 'Only, knowing him, I'll take bets he won't have the guts to do it.'

'Was I asked, which I don't conclude it's likely I will be,' declared the taller swamper in an amused cackle. 'I'd reckon he's lucky happen he's still got any guts, what you done to him, ma'am. Come on, Sonny, let's you 'n' me haul him into the alley.'

'Sure thing, Young 'N',' the shorter replied, showing a similar enthusiasm. 'Then, while he's coming 'round to get told, I reckon the boss-lady'll be wanting us to fetch buckets 'n' mops to clean off his leavings.'

' "Sonny", "Young 'N' "?' Madam queried, looking at Turner, as the elderly pair left without waiting to find out whether the suggestion met with her approval.

'We couldn't think of any other names which suited them *better*,' the bartender explained, the twinkle in his eyes matching the delighted beams on the faces of the remaining employees. 'It doesn't make Viola and the other gals blush like if we was to call them the Two Old Farts. Top of which, did we call them any such thing, they'd be like' to whomp us up good.'

'Urgh!' the blonde ejaculated, seeing she was being subjected to universally cheerful grins. Making a wry face, she went on in mock exasperation, 'I'm starting to figure out why Maxie was so all-fired willing to stake this place on a flush when he knew I was holding a full house. Talking of which, Joe, I don't see anybody who looks like a gambler.'

'No, boss,' the bartender admitted. 'There wasn't none of them around when we went to see Lawyer Scrope.'

'Some of these boys weren't around then, either,' Madam pointed out. 'But you sent for them and they came.'

'Yes'm!' Turner grunted non-committally.

'Are the gambling crew something *special*?' the blonde challenged.

'Might be you'd call them that, ma'am,' the bar-

53

tender said quietly and eyed the buxom woman in a speculative fashion. 'Didn't Maxie tell you—?'

'He told me there was gambling done here.'

'Nothing else?'

'How much "*else*" is there for him to have told?' Madam asked, then realized she had heard no mention of an important member of the staff. 'Who's floor boss when Maxie's not around?'

'We don't have one,' the bartender replied.

'Why not?'

'Mrs. Higgins was never so willing for him to throw his money around that she'd let him take one on. Or, happen she'd come to figuring there was a need, likely she'd have fetched in one of her kin to do it.'

'I don't have any kin to fetch in,' Madam declared and a brief suggestion of emotion crossed her face as she continued, 'Not that I'm in what could be called close touch with, anyways. Still, I don't reckon I'll be needing to look for one.'

'No, ma'am?' Turner asked, being a trifle disappointed as—having been performing the duties since the departure of Maxwell Higgins—he had hoped to be offered the position.

'Why should I be needing one?' the blonde asked with a smile. 'Or are you going to walk out on me now I've made *you* floor boss?'

'*Me*?' Turner gasped, hearing mutters of approval from the other members of the staff.

'Hell, you look the best of a worthless bunch,' Madam stated in mock disdain, satisfied she had made a popular selection. 'And now, seeing's how you're not one of the hired help any more and us bosses've got to stick together, you don't need to keep on being all shy and bashful about telling me what some of them are up to. Just how much more "*else*" do you reckon Maxie should have told me about the gambling men he hires?'

'That's just it, boss,' the newly appointed floor

54

manager answered. '*Maxie* didn't hire them. At least, not them's are running the games now.'

'How do you mean, *now*?'

'Just over a week back, a jasper called Leo Wallace showed up with a letter signed by Maxie saying's how he was to take over all the gambling.'

'Was it genuine?'

'Lawyer Scrope allowed the signature was, so far as he could tell, and Mrs. Higgins, her being there with Wallace, allowed everything else was as well.'

'Maxie didn't tell me anything about it, nor even that he was married,' Madam declared, the game of poker in which the saloon changed hands having taken place six days ago. 'Did you get told why this Wallace jasper was being let take over?'

'Seems like he's half-brother to Mrs. Higgins and asked for it,' Turner replied. 'Which being, Lawyer Scrope concluded there wasn't nothing could be done, 'cepting like Maxie said and let him take over. He'd brought some men with him and just yesterday his own faro table was fetched in. He's already started to pay off the old gambling crew.'

'Weren't they running straight games?'

'*They* were.'

'But those jaspers Wallace brought in aren't?'

'Nobody's *caught* any of them cheating,' Turner answered, glancing around and finding approval on the faces of his fellow workers. 'Which I can't set up as any kind of expert on such things. Even if I was, they've never left the cards, dice, dealing boxes, nor anything else's could be toted off at night around when they're not here so's I could take a closer look.'

'Somebody had better do i—!' Madam began, realizing why the three men had been using a tumbler instead of a dice cup when she arrived.

'Joe didn't hold back 'cause he was scared, boss!' Viola put in. 'But his missus's just had a baby and, well, Mrs. Higgins has backed up Wallace every time

55

he's said anybody should be fired. Which's always after they'd showed nosey about the gambling.'

'If it's a boy, I sure hope it doesn't grow up ugly like it's pappy,' the blonde remarked, making sure nobody believed she had harboured doubts about the courage or willingness of her new floor manager to take risks in the performance of his duty. 'Anyways, I said, "Somebody had better", not "Somebody should have" and, rank having its privileges, I'm the one who's going to do it as soon's——!'

Before Madam could finish, there was a knock on the door giving access to the bar-room.

'They're here and setting up, Joe!' announced the second of the waiters who had been present when the new owner arrived, stepping into the office.

'Just them?' the floor manager asked.

'He's not here yet,' the waiter replied.

'It's Wallace's men, boss,' Turner explained. 'Him and Mrs. Higgins went over to the county seat, her having more friends there than here. But I'd a notion you'd be wanting to look over the gamblers and the games as soon as they got here, whether he'd come back or not.'

CHAPTER FIVE

I'm Counting On You *Losing*

'Howdy there, boys,' greeted the new owner of the Hide And Horn Saloon, halting at the operating and well patronized table which was equipped for the game of faro. 'The name's Madam Bulldog and I reckon by now you'll likely all have heard I've won this place from Maxie Higgins in a poker game?'

'We've heard,' agreed one of the players, whose attire suggested he was a local businessman of moderate means, and the others mumbled concurrence with a similar lack of enthusiasm.

'How're you doing?' the buxom blonde inquired, although she could guess.

'Lousy!' answered the businessman. 'Ain't none of us can call a god-damned card right tonight!'

Having delayed only for long enough to explain to the members of the staff collected by Joseph Turner how she meant to have things done, Madam Bulldog had followed them from the private office. While they were scattering to their various duties, she and her newly appointed floor manager had looked around the bar-room. As she had anticipated, business had now vastly improved upon what it was when she had first arrived that afternoon. There was no sign of Town Marshal Tune Collier, or his elderly deputy, but Lawyer P. Scrope was seated at a table with half a dozen prosperous looking men she assumed to be among the leading citizens of Tennyson and who had been brought to make her acquaintance.

Although aware of how important it was to make a favourable impression upon them, the blonde had not gone across to the table of the attorney and his companions. Instead, saying she would commence her examination of the gambling games at the one which had been brought in most recently by Leo Wallace, she had asked Turner to tell them she would join them in a short while and hoped they would consider themselves her guests for the evening. She had felt sure that, unless her judgement of their character was at fault, they would be flattered by the invitation and lose any resentment which the delay in joining them might otherwise have aroused.

Judging from the far from amiable response to her greeting, the blonde considered she had reached a wise decision in making the faro game her first objective!

As far as appearances went, the table to which Madam made her way was apparently designed to be sufficiently sturdy to stand up to heavy usage. Its top, covered by a tiger decorated green baise cloth, also bearing the layout upon which bets of various kinds could be indicated, was some four inches thick and seemed to be solid timber. The faro game was supervised by a shortish, plump and flashily dressed dealer. He was assisted by a case-keeper who was clearly related to him and probably a twin brother, sharing a similar taste in clothes.

With his vision shaded and helped by a green eyeshade, the dealer was producing cards from a small box. Specially made for the purpose, this prevented the deck from being removed out of the top. Instead, a spring at the base held it firmly against the upper part of the frame and, having been loaded through the open rear, each individual card could be extracted through a narrow slot at the front. Equipped with a device like an abacus, except that it carried—as convention demanded, although the suits themselves had no significance in the play—pictures of the thirteen spade cards and there were four sliding wooden balls on a wire below each symbol, the case-keeper kept a record of every card as it was brought from the box.[1]

'And I'm right pleased to hear you can't,' the blonde informed the players, with a disarming cheerfulness and although this was not the case. 'Hell, fellers, I'm counting on you *losing* to help keep me in the manner to which I'm real willing to become accustomed.'

'We're doing that all right!' another of the players, a cowhand, stated as he was watching the final card of the deck leaving the box and the case-keeper began to help the dealer to collect the unsuccessful wagers. 'At least at the table's used to be here I got around to winning some of the time.'

'Is that so?' Madam inquired. 'Well, this's only my first day here and *everything* is new to me. So I reckon I'd better start sweetening you boys up a mite to make sure you keep coming back and losing more. Tell you what I'm going to do, I'm going to give this old dealing box a rub and see happen I can make your luck turn better.'

Having walked forward while speaking until standing alongside the dealer, the blonde reached out to pluck the receptacle in question from his grasp without giving him a chance to comment. Starting to do as she promised, by rubbing its base against the left sleeve of her jacket, it slipped from her right hand. Letting out a moderately profane exclamation of annoyance, she appeared to be compounding her clumsiness by stepping upon and crushing the sides of the box in her haste to retrieve it.

'God damned if just taking over's not making me all thumbs tonight!' Madam ejaculated, bending and picking up the ruined container. Then she swung what

1. *More detailed information about how the game of faro is played can be found in:* RANGELAND HERCULES. *J.T.E.*

seemed to be a guileless gaze to the dealer. His face was registering a much greater annoyance than the incident appeared to warrant, particularly when the cause of the accident was also the owner of the saloon and, ostensibly, his new employer. With her voice taking on something very much like a timbre of apology, she continued, 'Sorry, but it looks like I've busted this son-of-a-bitch to hell and gone. Oh well, hang the expense, get another out of the drawer down there. Only this time pick one with just a finger hole and not an open top. They don't get all scrunched up so easy, should they get stepped on.'

'*Drawer*?' the flashily dressed man inquired sullenly, but his pretense at ignorance was far from convincing and, although there was no sign of such a fitment being included in the table, he could not prevent himself from throwing a hurried glance downwards before going on, 'What drawer'd that be?'

'Maybe the layout's too new for you to know about it?' the blonde suggested, still seemingly amicable and eager to help. Pointing at the thick end of the table nearest to her and the dealer, she elaborated, 'That drawer in there!'

'I don't—!' the man began.

'One thing you'd best get to know about me from the start, which's *now*,' Madam warned and, despite her apparently bland expression, there was a discernible hardening of her tone. 'I'm the kind of *boss* who expects to have *everything* I tell done straight away and without arguing.'

'But—!' the dealer commenced, turning a worried look towards the case-keeper who was his younger brother by about thirty minutes and was showing an equal consternation.

'Was I you Fletcher boys,' Turner commented. 'I'd do just what the boss-lady tells you!' Having delivered the message and having it accepted with gratitude by the attorney's party, he had come across to the faro table in time to hear the latter part of the conversation. Halting alongside his new employer, ready to support her even though he was not certain in what, he dipped his right hand into the pocket of the jacket he had donned before leaving for the interview with the lawyer and in which he was carrying a short, leather-wrapped, spring-loaded sap he used to help the bouncers when necessary. Although he grasped it, he did not bring it into view as he spoke.

Ever since the table had been installed in place of its much less sturdily constructed predecessor, the floor manager had suspected it was less innocuous than it appeared externally. However, as he had been awaiting the return of Maxwell Higgins before deciding whether to remain, or quit the saloon and seek employment elsewhere, he had not attempted to satisfy his curiosity. He had realized that, should his assumptions prove correct—as he had anticipated was probably the case—he would be asking for trouble if he had made them known. Now, confident he had an employer who would back his play in return, he was willing to take risks by supporting her.

Exchanging another brief glance with his brother, who replied with an uninformative shrug, the dealer next darted a hurried look around the bar-room. There were several men present who, as was the case with him and his sibling, had been brought to Tennyson by Leo Wallace. The primary purpose of two of these was to prevent such unwelcome instructions being enforced. However, at that moment, both were fully occupied with members of the saloon's staff elsewhere and he could not think of any safe way to attract their attention. What was more, knowing the gamblers had made themselves unpopular with the other workers, he felt disinclined to provoke an incident which would almost certainly lead to violence. Neither he nor his brother were naturally aggressive or courageous and, if the behaviour of Turner was anything to go by, the new owner had already acquired at least one ally willing to stand up for her.

'Sure, Joe,' the dealer mumbled, having made his brief summation of the situation and not cared for its conclusions. 'If that's the way *you* want it!'

'*Me* my ass!' Turner corrected, refusing to grant Abel Fletcher even that much of a face-saver. 'That's the way the *boss-lady* wants it and what she says goes for *everybody* who works in here!'

'Come on, blast it, all this talk's holding these good old boys from doing some more losing,' Madam went on, waving a hand towards the interested—albeit, clearly puzzled—players. Then, exuding an obvious and definite authority for the first time, she ordered, 'So open up the drawer and get out a fresh box, or I'll have to ask around for somebody who knows where it is and will.'

Flickering another worried look about him, the dealer found the two hard-cases were still engaged in their respective activities and neither were so much as glancing his way. Not entirely disappointed by the discovery, considering it absolved himself and his brother of all blame for obeying, he directed a shrug of resignation to his sibling. Receiving a gesture signifying an equal acceptance of the circumstances from Cain, their parents having had a taste for biblical names—although some people might have considered the choice a strange selection—he yielded to the inevitable.

Despite his protestations of ignorance, Abel reached to press a switch disguised as a knot in the wood and caused a carefully concealed drawer to open. As he was putting his hand inside, he gazed for a moment at the three dealing boxes and half a dozen identical looking decks of cards it held. Then he realized the blonde was in all probability aware that the differences in their construction were not merely intended to grant an increased resistance to damage if stepped upon. Therefore, he took out one with only a small hole in the centre of the lid and left the others which, like the example she had destroyed—deliberately, he now felt certain—had the whole of the top left open apart from a small rim.

'That's just the kind I want,' Madam confirmed, being able to see the entire contents of the drawer and having noticed the slight hesitancy in making the selection. 'And, seeing as how we're trying to change these boys here's luck, you might as well give them a *clean* deck while you're at it.'

'A *new* deck?' the dealer suggested, aware of the connotation amongst professional gamblers which was implied by the word, "clean".

'Hell, why not?' the blonde challenged, adopting an air of jovial recklessness. 'A doctor I've sat in games with on occasion, feller called Holliday and he was really a dentist when he worked at it,[2] always said dirty cards are plumb unhealthy. So let's go hang with the expense. Throw that deck you've been using away and hand me another one from the drawer. I'll break the seal personally and give the deck a stack with my own lily white hands for luck.'

Repeating the shrug of resignation, the dealer placed the box on the table and, having tossed the cards with which the game had been played on to the floor, took an unopened deck from the drawer. They would, as he had been instructed, qualify for the required 'cleanliness'. Not that, he told himself with gloomy satisfaction, the fact that they were devoid of secret marks denoting their value to him, be of any further importance under the circumstances.

To make use of a marked deck when playing faro, a 'second dealer' box was necessary. Unlike the one which the elder of the Fletcher twins was now being compelled to operate, wherein almost all of the uppermost card's back was concealed and there being a slot only sufficiently wide for it to pass through alone, the

2. *If this was the notorious gambler and gun fighter, John H. 'Doc' Holliday, we have no record of where Madam Bulldog made his acquaintance. J.T.E.*

slit in a cheating device was open enough to permit at least two to be moved out. Having the majority of the top removed to allow the secret markings to be visible to the dealer, the box ruined by the blonde was of the latter variety. When in use, should the markings indicate the card on top was unfavourable to the 'house', it could be retracted by a skiful manipulator and one more suitable be put into play.

Handing the ruined second dealer box to Turner, instead of returning it to the table, Madam took off and tucked her gloves into the right side pocket of the travelling costume's jacket. Then, accepting the wrapped packet which was being offered to her by Abel Fletcher with a suggestion of reluctance, she broke it open with her thumb and extracted the cards. Removing and tossing aside the jokers, she held the rest firmly in her left hand—which was devoid of rings—and bent them at the top with her right thumb. Watching them carefully, as they were being allowed to return one after another in rapid succession to the upright position, she allowed them to slip free from the thumb in a riffling motion.

Whatever lingering doubts might have been held by the dealer and case-keeper, with regards to the knowledge of such matters possessed by the new owner, were quickly dispelled by her latest behaviour. Being experienced in cheating methods themselves, they were not taken in by her apparently casual treatment of the cards. Abel, in particular, felt relieved over having decided against disobeying the demand she had made for a clean deck. By watching the design on the backs of the rapidly moving cards, she was carrying out a test for detecting a marked deck. If they had been treated in any such fashion, the kaleidoscopic effect of the movement would have caused slight variations in the pattern instead of it remaining constant.

'There you go, boys,' Madam announced, having completed the shuffling of the deck with a flambouyant style and manual dexterity reminiscent of a magician specializing in sleight of hand. 'All stacked neat and lucky with my own dainty lil fingers. Have them cut by somebody and put in the box, Mr. Dealer-Man. Then let's see happen we've done something to change these good old boys' luck for them.'

'Yes'm!' Abel assented gloomily, accepting there was nothing to the contrary he and his brother could do at that moment.

'I reckon you Fletcher boys will soon enough come around to *my* way of thinking about which kind of box's better,' the blonde went on, having no qualms due to the sight of the cards she had shuffled being placed in a legitimate dealing receptacle. 'Happen you stick around long enough, that is.'

Clearly, Abel concluded—as he exchanged quick looks with his brother and detected a similar understanding of exactly what had been implied by the remark—the new owner did not intend to allow her customers to be cheated by Leo Wallace's employees. Furthermore, at least where cards were concerned, she had proven herself sufficiently well informed to detect attempts to do so and, in all probability, would be equally knowledgeable concerning the other games such as chuck-a-luck. However, regardless of the house having an advantageous percentage which ensured a steady income from every game of chance it operated, their actual employer had always insisted upon the use of dishonest means to increase the profits.

The dealer wondered how Wallace, a far from meek and compliant man given adequate backing, would react when he heard there was to be a change of policy?

CHAPTER SIX

I Was Just *Lucky*, I Guess

Having delivered what the dealer and the case-keeper knew to be a warning, Madam Bulldog retrieved the gloves from her pocket and donned them. She was satisfied that, for the time being, at least, there was no further need on her part for supervision of the faro table. What she had done would render any more cheating impossible as, she felt confident, the Fletcher brothers would not chance substituting another second dealer box and deck of marked cards from the concealed drawer until they had seen what took place between herself and Leo Wallace. Therefore, reaching out with her left hand and taking the ruined receptacle from Joseph Turner, she turned away without waiting to watch the play being resumed.

'I didn't know there was a drawer down there, boss,' Turner apologised, feeling he might be considered remiss in having failed to make the discovery and holding his voice to a level which would not reach the players he and the buxom blonde were leaving.

'It was damned well hidden, so don't blame yourself,' Madam replied. 'I expected there would be one, though. There mostly is when the top of the table's that thick.'

'Are you going to fire the Fletcher boys?' the floor manager inquired.

'Would you?' the blonde consulted.

66

'They're not such ornery sons-of-bitches as some's Wallace brought in with him, and they know how to handle the table. A good faro crew's not easy to find.'

'Then it all depends on *them*. They'll likely be smart enough to spot cheating from the outside as well as doing it themselves. So, happen they're willing to play straight all the time and say they want to, I'd be willing to keep them on.'

'Do you want to tell them, or shall I?'

'You can do it, like you're doing them a favour, then send them to see me. But it'll wait until later.'

'You handled things back there real well, boss,' Turner praised. 'What with that goddamned table showing up just the day before you arrived to say you're taking over, it's likely you'd've been blamed and not Leo Wallace had anybody been slick enough to figure out how they were being cheated.'

'Something of the sort did cross my mind,' the blonde admitted with a smile, pleased and flattered by the frank admiration the burly man was showing. 'Is there anybody else from around town you reckon I should know about, before we go and meet those high mucky-mucks Counselor Scrope's fetched in to show me off to?'

'None of the ranchers are in tonight,' Turner replied. Glancing around, he discovered that Viola Grant and the bartender who had announced the arrival of the gambling staff were turning away from the two hard-cases they had been distracting ever since they had seen their new employer making for the suspect faro table. Pleased they had shown such a ready grasp of the situation and were willing to supply their support unasked, he noticed somebody he felt qualified to be mentioned. 'There's that bunch over at the *vingt-un* table.'

Following the direction surreptitiously indicated by her floor manager, also without making the interest obvious, Madam studied the half a dozen obvious town dwellers to whom he had referred. Wise in such matters, sensing Turner did not hold them in very high esteem, she deduced who was the most likely candidate to be their leader. Tall and thickset, albeit running to fat, the man was swarthily handsome in a florid fashion and clearly had a high opinion of himself. He was dressed in the kind of loud check suit and derby hat frequently worn by travelling salesmen, particularly those dealing in cheaper brands of liquor. However, she felt it unlikely this was his present occupation.

'Who are they?' the blonde asked.

'The jasper dressed so quiet and tasteful's Josh Gilmore,' Turner supplied. 'He owns the blacksmith's forge.'

'He doesn't look much like the poem says,' Madam commented.

'That's because he won the smithy from the feller's owned it in a poker game,' the floor manager explained, being equally conversant with the piece of verse by Henry Wadsworth Longfellow.[1] 'And the same feller's doing all the work there, reckoning on one day getting it back the same way.'

'How about the rest?'

'They're his cronies and butt-lickers. Either own or work in different places around town and reckon they're a real sporting bunch, what with running dog fights, cock fights, fist fights and such in the Barnhof Saloon. That's owned by Rudolf Schanz, the fat, middle sized *hombre* rigged out like a Mississippi riverboat gambling man.'

---

1. THE VILLAGE BLACKSMITH, *(1842) by Henry Wadsworth Longfellow.*

> *Under the spreading chestnut tree,*
> *The village smithy stands,*
> *The smith, a mighty man is he,*
> *With large and sinewy hands,*
> *And the muscles of his brawny arms,*
> *Are strong as iron bands.*

'Maxie told me there were a couple more saloons in town.'

'Sure, but neither of them're near here and they don't pull in so much trade as we do, being on the Square.'

'I'm right pleased to hear *that*,' Madam declared with a smile. 'Not's I'm scared of having fair competition, mind.'

'They're neither of them any competition,' the floor manager asserted. 'But, should there be any from Schanz, I wouldn't count on it being *fair*, was I you.'

'Has Maxie had trouble with him?'

'Nope.'

'Has Schanz or the other owner got cause for complaint over us being here?' the blonde asked, knowing the erection of a new establishment could cause resentment on the part of the owners of older businesses.

'Not on account of them being here longer, happen that's what you mean,' Turner replied. 'The Hide And Horn Saloon's the oldest in town.'

'So Maxie got on all right with Schanz and the other owner?'

'You know Maxie, he could get on with most folks. Used to get invited to whatever sporting doings's Schanz had going—But only when Gilmore wasn't figuring on being there.'

'So he didn't get on with Gilmore?'

'Let's put it this way, boss,' the floor manager suggested. 'Gilmore got on with Mrs. Higgins in a way that's a whole heap cosier 'n' safer done when the husband's not around. Only, word has it, just recent' she's been tending to favour Lloyd Bowman. He's——!'

'County sheriff and mostly stays down to Garnett,' Madam interrupted and, although interested in what she had been told, as it helped her to form a clearer picture of the local situation and events which might affect her ownership of the Hide And Horn Saloon,

69

she went on with a grin, 'Lordy lord. And they do say it's us women who gossip!'

'Well, ma'am, so far as that goes,' Turner replied, as seriously as if imparting advice of great importance. 'My old daddy allus used to tell me, "Son, women *gossip*, but us men pass out *news* as is helpful." '

'My old momma allus used to tell me, "Don't hire a feller who gets smart-assed",' the blonde warned, mimicking the floor manager's Texas drawl. Reverting to her normal voice, she continued, 'Come on, Joe. We'd best wander on over and say, "Howdy, you-all". I reckon that's what they're here for.'

'And to get some free drinks,' Turner supplemented, starting to accompany his employer towards the *vingt-un* table in a leisurely fashion.

However, the intention of Madam Bulldog to greet Joshua Gilmore and his cronies met with a delay!

Coming across to the blonde and her newly appointed floor manager, the cowhand who had acted as her porter, thanked her for her generosity. She noticed it did not appear he had abused her hospitality by indulging too lavishly in the free drinks. Certainly there was no suggestion of drunkeness in his voice as he asked if she would, 'Meet the boys from my spread'. Aware of how important it was to establish suitably friendly relationships with all her customers and avoid letting it seem she regarded some as more worthy of attention than others lower on the social scale, she agreed.

However, as Madam and Turner were being escorted to where four younger and cheerful looking cowhands were sharing a table with the saloongirl, Bottles, she sensed there might be something more to the invitation than appeared upon the surface. Not serious trouble, such as a direct challenge to her authority, nor a desire to prove that they considered themselves superior to a woman, even if she did own a saloon. Certainly they were not showing signs of drunken truculence and hostility. Rather they were studying her in an amiable and even admiring fashion. Then three of them and the artificial blonde started to gaze at the fourth of the group in an expectant fashion. Shoving his chair away and hanging his hat on its back, he rose and confronted the owner.

'Howdy, you-all, Madam Bulldog ma'am. I'm Curly from the Leaning J. Me'n the boys here was wondering if you're of a sporting nature?'

'Well, yes, I reckon you just might say I am at that, fellers,' the buxom blonde admitted, satisfied that the joviality of the party was caused by high rather than intoxicating spirits. However, despite the question having been addressed to her in a polite and respectful manner, she noticed that she was being watched by everybody in the vicinity, and her instincts warned she was once again about to be subjected to a test of some kind. What was more, judging from his attitude, she concluded that Turner knew what it was going to be. Satisfied from his reaction that it would not prove too serious or embarrassing, she went on, 'So what'd your pleasure be, Curly, cards or Indian wrestling?'

'Why cards, for sure, ma'am,' the young cowhand replied, running fingers through dark hair which indicated how his sobriquet had arisen and speaking somewhat louder than was necessary just to be heard by the new owner of the saloon. 'I mind the last time I Indian wrestled, I——!'

'Won the Indian,' Madam finished before the speaker could, also raising her voice for the benefit of the attentive audience.

'By cracky, ma'am!' chuckled the former porter, clearly amused—as were the rest of the listeners, including the victim—to see Curly circumvented. 'You called her just the way she happened!'

'And it wasn't even what you'd call a *pretty* Indian he won,' another of the Leaning J ranch's contingent went on.

'I don't reckon I'd want an Indian, pretty or not,' the blonde asserted. 'So what's it to be, *amigo*, poker?'

'I'd admire to take a whirl at that, ma'am,' Curly declared, showing no animosity over having his favourite joke taken away from him. 'Only I don't reckon, you being on your first night here's boss and all, you've got over much time to spare for playing poker.'

'Do you have something else in mind?' Madam hinted.

Nodding in eager confirmation, Curly dipped his right hand into the side pocket of the loose fitting jacket he was wearing. He brought out a wooden laundry clothespin and five playing cards, spreading out the latter so they were overlapping in a straight line. Turning them face upwards, he showed there were two low spades on either side of the queen of diamonds.

'Now this here's the idea for the game, ma'am,' the cowhand explained. 'I turn these five cards face downwards without changing how they lay and all you have to do is grab hold of the lil ole red gal in the middle here with the clothespin.'

'Sounds like we're back to the Indians again,' Madam claimed. 'Is that *all* there is to it, then?'

'That's every last thing you have to do, ma'am,' Curly confirmed, trading a knowing grin with his companions. 'Just reach out and snap that ole clothespin on the lil red lady. Which hand you do it with don't make no never-mind at all to me.'

'What's the name of this game?' the blonde inquired, shaking her head in a manner suggesting puzzlement.

'It's called, "Pick With A Clothespin" back where I come from, ma'am,' the cowhand asserted. 'Do you fancy chancing your hand at doing it?'

'By cracky, yes!' Madam agreed enthusiastically. 'If that's *all* there is to it, damned if I don't up and give it a whirl!'

'You wouldn't be wanting to put up a dollar's says you can clothespin that ole queen, now would you, ma'am?'

'Just a dollar?'

'We *could* make it for more, was *you* so minded, ma'am,' Curly offered, but without undue enthusiasm, as he was uncertain of how the new owner would react on taking the loss which had never failed to occur when he played the game with others. 'I'll just leave it up to you.'

'That being, I reckon one simoleon will suit me just fine,' Madam claimed and, having borrowed a silver dollar from Turner, laid it on the table. 'I'm only a poor saloonkeeper who can't even afford to carry that much about with her, not one of your rich cattle kings.'

'Well, I can't say's how I've made the vast fortune which I so richly deserves just yet, ma'am,' Curly countered, rotating his right hand until the cards were facing downwards and offering the clothespin with the left. 'But this might just be the start of it.'

'I'm all for helping out a right deserving young feller to start making his vast fortune,' the blonde declared, accepting the pin. 'But not with *my* money. So here goes a try for the queen!'

Having made the declaration, Madam extended her right hand. However, instead of allowing the open jaws of the clothespin to close upon the card which now appeared to be in the centre, she gripped the one on the right with them. Extracting all five without difficulty from the suddenly unresisting fingers of the young cowhand, whose jaw had dropped until his mouth hung open, she raised them so their faces could be seen.

Due to the discrepancy in the way the cards were positioned, whether face uppermost or downwards, the blonde proved to be holding the queen and not, as would have happened if she had selected the one apparently in the centre, the low spade at the end.

'Well, I'll be *damned*!' Curly ejaculated, after staring for a moment and the onlookers, many of whom had fallen for the trick in the past, began to laugh at his dumbfounded confusion. 'You—You—!'

'By golly, ma'am!' whooped the former porter. 'You nailed him on that one as well!'

'I was just *lucky*, I guess,' Madam replied, returning the cards, still held by the clothespin, to their discomforted and yet not annoyed owner. Then, picking up the dollar and holding it between her right thumb and forefinger, she showed each of its sides to him and continued, 'Tell you what, though, Curly.'

'Yes'm?'

'Seeing as how I wouldn't want to go down in history as the one who slowed you from making your vast fortune, I'll give you a chance to get this and your own simoleon back. You put up another dollar against them, I'll flip it—and give you two guesses.'

'*Two* guesses?'

'Surely you don't expect me to give you more than the *two*?'

'Well, no, ma'am. But—!'

'Are you on?' Madam demanded, with an air of issuing a challenge.

'Happen *you're* happy with it that way, ma'am,' Curly assented, sounding less than excited, despite having been offered such favourable terms for guessing the result of the spinning of a coin. Considering luck, rather than intelligence or skill, had caused him to lose the hitherto always successful trick, he found this disappointing because he had formed a respect as well as a liking for the new owner. Nevertheless, he went on, 'It's a bet!'

'Up she goes then!' the blonde announced, flipping the coin with her thumb so it rose spinning into the air. Catching it as it started to fall and slapping it on to the table concealed by her hand, she asked, 'What *year* is it?'

'Hea——!' Curly began instinctively, before the realization of how the question had been worded struck him.

'I've never heard of a year called, "heads",' Madam stated. 'So that's your first guess gone wrong.'

74

'Well, by cracky, ma'am!' whooped one of the Leaning J cowhands, while the others and rest of the onlookers were showing an equal amusement. 'You've done roped and throwed ole Curly again!'

'That's for sure and I'm yelling calf-rope!' the victim conceded, his tone rueful without showing the slightest trace of anger. 'But I sure wish you'd've pulled that one on me when there wasn't so many of these jaspers watching. That way, I could've used it against them.'

'You should've told me that *before* I did it,' Madam pointed out, employing a kind of illogical logic which she felt sure would appeal to the sense of humour of the listening cowhands. 'Anyways, leave it not be said in history books that I stopped a promising young man starting to make the vast fortune he deserves on my first night in the Hide And Horn Saloon. Let me set up drinks with the winnings for you boys. Only don't go getting Bottles there liquored. I've heard she can get real mean on occasion.'

'Only when I reckon I can lick the other gal with Vi and Sally backing me, boss,' the artificial blonde declared, deciding her new employer was a good sport and bore no malice over her earlier behaviour.

' "Pick With A Clothespin" indeed,' Madam said to Turner, as they moved away from the table. However, he noticed there was none of the derision or rancour which his former employer had frequently used when referring to this most numerous group of customers. 'Cowhands', she went on, 'It's been a coon's age since I last saw anybody try to pull the old monte-plus game. Lordy lord, it makes me feel *old*. I was about Curly's age back when Joe Brambile took me with it and showed me how it worked.'[2]

---

2. *Some modern practitioners of the confidence trick called 'monte-plus' use a stationery bulldog clip to hold the cards. The trick has no connection whatsoever, except where the name is concerned, with the gambling card game, 'Spanish monte'; details of which are given in:* THE SHERIFF OF ROCKABYE COUNTY. *J.T.E.*

'I hope you'll show *me* how it works,' the floor manager confessed, having been one of the young cowhand's victims and knowing the man named by his employer to have been a successful and respected professional gambler for a great many years.[3] He considered she had made a very good impression upon all who had witnessed the incident and felt sure they would spread her praises when leaving. 'Because I still haven't figured out how the sucker works, even after seeing it licked.'

'I'll show you some time,' Madam promised. 'But right now, we'd best get on over to the village blacksmith and his bunch, so's I can go and meet Counsel—!'

'Boss!' Turner breathed urgently, having glanced at the main entrance. 'Leo Wallace's just come in!'

3. *Information about some of the career of professional gambler, Joseph Brambile can be found in:* DOC LEROY, M.D. *and Part Two, 'Jordan's Try', THE TOWN TAMERS. J.T.E.*

CHAPTER SEVEN

I've *Never* Heard of You

Hearing the announcement delivered *sotto voce* by her newly appointed floor manager, Madam Bulldog turned her attention from an examination of Joshua Gilmore and his cronies so she could look in the direction indicated. The group of townsmen were still by the *vingt-un* table, but no longer playing. They had been watching what had taken place between her and Curly of the Leaning J ranch. Now, unless she was mistaken, she was the subject of a conversation which she felt certain she would not have found complimentary if overheard.

'I'm real pleased that he's come,' the buxom blonde declared, putting the activities of the group from her mind for the moment. 'The sooner we get things settled between us about how the gambling's going to be run in here from now on, the better I'll be satisfied.'

'Shall I fetch Lawyer Scrope?' Joseph Turner suggested, knowing that the verification of proof of ownership might be called for.

'Not just yet,' Madam decided, subjecting the person under discussion to a careful scrutiny which, nevertheless, was far from obvious. Being wise in such matters, she considered that the other members of the local community present would be more adequately impressed if she did not call upon the services of a member of the legal profession; even one so well liked as Aloysius P. Scrope. 'Let's see happen we can settle this ourselves, without needing to cut in the Counsellor and his important friends.'

'What do you reckon to Wallace, boss?' the floor manager inquired.

'I suppose his mother *might* have loved him, happen he was *all* she had to choose from,' the blonde replied, noticing that the man who was the subject of their conversation was sauntering towards them in a leisurely fashion as if wishing to emphasise his independence and importance. 'Come on, Joe. Let's go and meet him half way, seeing that's what he has in mind.'

Taken all in all, especially in view of the influence he had been allowed to exercise over the gambling side of the business at the Hide And Horn Saloon in the absence of its previous owner, Madam did not consider Leo Wallace to be a very impressive or imposing figure. About five foot six inches in height, with pallid and rat-like features, he had reddish hair which straggled untidily from beneath a wide brimmed and low crowned black hat. Skinny and narrow shouldered, dressed in what were obviously expensive clothes, he affected the style of a successful professional gambler. He was armed with a short barrelled, nickel plated Colt Navy Model of 1851 revolver, which had a mother of pearl handle, in a cross draw holster on the left side of a well polished black gunbelt.

'He's got some working for him who're plenty tougher than the Fletcher boys,' Turner warned, nodding rearwards towards the faro table and contriving to be audible while barely moving his lips. 'Which's who-all he's wig-wagging to right now.'

'I figured that was what he's up to,' the blonde admitted, having noticed the gestures to left and right made by the man with whom she was expecting a confrontation. Avoiding the slightest indication of having seen anything of the possible danger, despite having located to whom the signals were made, she went on, 'Remind me to thank Vi and Sam for keeping those two hard-cases out of my hair while I was 'tending to the Fletcher boys.'

'You saw them, huh?' the floor manager queried, having intended to bring the asistance given by the boss girl and waiter to the attention of his employer at a more convenient moment.

'It sort of took my eye,' Madam confirmed, directing another seemingly cursory look around and keeping the ruined second dealer box behind her back. Taking a few more steps, she came to a halt before the newcomer and greeted, 'Howdy there. Are you looking for me?'

'I reckon I could be,' Wallace admitted, as if conferring a favour.

'I'm not hiring, should you be looking for work,' the blonde declared amiably. 'But, should you be down on your luck, I reckon I can stake you to a meal and broke money.'[1]

'Broke money?' Wallace almost yelped, throwing a puzzled look at Turner and, despite the amusement caused by the suggestion, receiving only a blank stare. Wondering if his arrival in the bar-room had been overlooked, he returned his gaze to the speaker and went on with all the self importance he could muster. 'Don't you know who I am?'

'I can't say's I've had the *pleasure*,' Madam replied— truthfully, as far as it went—her manner suggesting she considered she was not speaking to anybody of consequence.

'The name's Leo Wallace!' the skinny gambler proclaimed,[2] rather than merely introduced, his manner

1. *'Broke money': a small sum, ostensibly to purchase a meal and transport home, supplied by the 'house' to players who have been consistent losers. J.T.E.*

2. *John Scarne—author of* SCARNE ON CARDS *and* SCARNE ON DICE, *arguably the world's foremost authority upon such matters—points out that, although providing a service in one form or another, the operator of games of chance in a saloon does not*

79

implying he had covered everything with the four words.

'Is that so?' the blonde queried, sounding far from impressed. 'Well, like I told you, Mr. Wallace, I still don't recollect having had the pleasure. Anyways, happen you aren't looking for work, what can I do for you?'

'Didn't Maxie tell you about me?' the gambler demanded.

'Is there any reason why he should have?' Madam inquired, exuding an innocence which appeared genuine.

'Ain't you her's reckons to have won the Hide And Horn offen him?'

'No!'

'*No*?'

Having concluded the business which had taken them to the county seat more quickly than was expected, Mrs. Wanda Higgins had ordered her half-brother to return to Tennyson and ensure the staff of the saloon were not interfering with the gambling side of the business. On hearing of the change in ownership on his arrival in town, he had come to investigate. However, despite the blonde fitting the description given by Moses Stern—who had refused to accompany him—the answer he had just received caused him to wonder if he had made an error when selecting her as the person he was seeking.

'*No!*' Madam reaffirmed, just as vehemently as the question had been posed. 'But I'm *her* who won the Hide And Horn from him, if that's what you mean!'

'*You* won it?' Wallace asked, as if unable to believe his ears.

'*I* won it,' the blonde stated.

---

actually gamble in the same way as the players. Therefore, technically, he does not qualify for the name, 'professional gambler'. However, to avoid confusion, we will continue to refer to Leo Wallace in that fashion. J.T.E.

'Does Wan—my sis—his *missus*—know about it?'
Wallace challenged, despite having sent a telegraph
message to the woman in question telling her the
news.

'I didn't even know Maxie had a wife,' Madam
claimed and, having only learned of the former owner's marital status since her arrival in Tennyson, she
was speaking something close to the truth. 'It never
came up while we were playing poker, nor when he
was signing over the deeds of the place to me after
he'd lost it.'

'How come Maxie lost out to *you*?' the gambler
growled, glancing to where his two toughest men
were approaching from opposite sides of the room. He
was confident the woman was unaware of their
presence. 'He's a helluva good poker player!'

'So am I,' the blonde replied, without offering to
dispute the statement regarding the ability of Maxwell
Higgins. 'Else we wouldn't neither of us have been sat
in on the Big One in the Silver Bell Saloon in
Cowtown, which's were he lost it to me.'

'The *Big One*?' Wallace repeated, wondering why the
blonde was keeping her right hand concealed behind
her back and taking comfort from the thought that his
two converging men would prevent her from using
any weapon she might be holding.

'The *Big One*,' Madam reiterated, with a similar
emphasis and continued, as if explaining to a far from
bright child. 'That's a poker game played in the Silver
Bell Saloon over to Fort Worth. They call it the "Big
One" because the stakes get high and—!'

'I know what the son-of-a-bitching Big One is!' the
gambler protested indignantly. Conscious of the silence which had descended upon the bar-room and
aware that everybody was paying full attention to
what was being said, he tried to dispel the suggestion
that he could be so lacking in knowledge. 'But I've
never heard tell of no *woman* being let sit in on the Big
One!'

81

'Then you can't have heard so all-fired much about it as you're *trying* to make out,' Madam declared, knowing the trend in the conversation taken by Wallace was intended to discredit her. 'There hasn't been too many of us, I'll have to admit. But Poker Alice was sitting in along with me that night and, at least so I was told, Madame Moustache had been one of the big winners the time before. Happen you *might* have heard of *them*, seeing's how you reckon to know so much about gambling.'

'Everybody's heard of them two!' Wallace claimed, the women in question having acquired reputations by virtue of their respective abilities as professional gamblers. They were well known to be welcome as participants wherever games for high stakes were played.[3] 'But I ain't never heard *nothing* about no "Madam Bulldog"!'

'And I've never heard of you, which makes us sort of even,' the blonde countered. Then her manner implied she was growing tired of the discussion and she went on, 'Anyways, Mr. *Wallace*, is it?—It's real pleasureable talking to you, but I'm more than a mite busy what with just having taken over from Maxie and all. So, while I'm sorry happen he offered you a job here. Right n—!'

'I'm not looking for any "mother-something" job!' the gambler corrected angrily. 'Wan—*Maxie* turned over the running of all the gambling to me!'

'To *you*?' Madam queried, sounding as if she could not credit the former owner with having done anything so obviously stupid.

'Yeah, to *me!*' Wallace insisted, although he knew he would have been more correct if he had completed his

3. *Further information regarding 'Poker Alice' and 'Madam Moustache' can be found in:* Part Two, 'The Gamblers', THE WILDCATS. *As we infer in,* CUT ONE, THEY ALL BLEED, *Calamity Jane was soon to be another female participant in the Big One.* J.T.E.

82

original sentence about who had granted him the permission.

'When did this happen?'

'Weeks back!'

'*Weeks* back?'

'Well, I only got here last week,' Wallace revised, realizing the length of the period he had quoted could be questioned. 'But it was all set for me to take over afore he lit out and I got here's fast's I could. Didn't he say *nothing* to you about it?'

'It must have slipped his mind, him having a heap more *important* things to be thinking about,' Madam asserted, seemingly devoting all her attention to the man with whom she was conversing. 'Now let me get the straights of this, Mr. Wallace. Your sist—Maxie— hired you to help out by looking after the gambling while he was away, huh?'

'*Looking after?*' the gambler almost squeaked, quivering with rage and wondering whether the blonde really was unaware of the arrangement, or was merely baiting him. Deciding it did not greatly matter which, although there would be an added pleasure from seeing her made to suffer if the latter should prove the case, he went on belligerently, 'Wand—*Maxie* said I was to *run* all the gambling and give him a cut of my take.'

'Is that so?' asked the blonde, conveying an impression of being distressed by the discovery. 'Then all the gambling gear in here belongs to you, huh?'

'Ye—!' Wallace began, then realized the claim could be disproved. 'Well, no!'

'So you don't own any of it?' Madam asked.

'The faro table's mine,' Wallace declared and, wanting to establish the fact that he had brought sufficient equipment to justify the kind of arrangement he claimed existed between himself and the former owner, he went on hurriedly, 'So's the cards, dice 'n' dice cups!'

'And the dealing boxes over to the faro layout?'

83

'Of course they're mine!'

'Then this must be yours,' the blonde suggested, in a seemingly mild and innocuous fashion, bringing her right hand into view.

'Yea—!' the gambler began, staring at the object exposed to his gaze. 'What the hell happened to it?'

'It got busted when I dropped it and stepped on it,' Madam explained, in something which might have passed as an apologetic tone. 'That's *one* trouble with *second dealer* boxes. They're a whole heap more fragile than "straights".'

'Is that so?' Wallace snarled, concluding from the use of the terms, "second dealer" and "straights" that the woman knew the purpose of each type of box and the destruction had not been accidental. Making a motion with his head, he continued, 'All right, you—!'

While the conversation had been taking place, the two men summoned by Wallace had been moving inwards. Big and burly, their attire was similar to his; albeit of a cheaper quality. However, as everybody present knew, their purpose was to act as bodyguards rather than workers at the gambling tables. Knowing there was likely to be trouble from the new owner, who did not appear to have heard of the arrangement between their employer and Mrs. Higgins, they were ready to help him protect his lucrative interests.

Right thumb hooked into his gunbelt close to the walnut butt of its Colt 1860 Army Model revolver, Barry Norman, the taller of the pair, was confronting Turner with a prohibitive scowl on his face. Herbert Lang had halted close behind the blonde. Having received the awaited signal from his employer, he was opening his arms and preparing to encircle hers.

The shorter hard-case discovered his presence was far from unexpected. Things were not as he had assumed!

Allowing the ruined second dealer box to slip from her grasp, Madam suddenly thrust her bent arm to the rear. Before Lang was able to complete the incapacitat-

84

ing hold from behind, the elbow rammed into his *solar plexus* with considerable force. Letting out a startled and pain filled gasping obscenity, he reeled backwards a few steps. Nor, although he was not affected directly, was this the only result of the unanticipated attack.

Hearing the thud, and the profanity croaked in a masculine voice, which suggested the victim was not a woman, Norman could not prevent an involuntary impulse to look around!

Similarly, finding one of his bodyguards had run into an unexpected difficulty, Wallace felt there was a need to take some form of action himself!

Neither met with any success!

Having surmised his new employer might be far less oblivious of the danger than was apparent, a belief increased by watching how she was treating Wallace, the floor manager was ready to back whatever play she made. Without having aroused any protest from Norman, who was engrossed in looking at his companion, he had returned his right hand to his pocket and was once more grasping the sap.

Immediately the gaze of the hard-case was turned from him, Turner brought out the weapon. Instead of aiming at the top of the skull, which was adequately protected by the broad brimmed hat, he swung the sap across and upwards. Gaining power from the whip-like action of the spring in the handle, the lead loaded head met the jaw of the man as his gaze was returning to the front. Being stunned, his hand missed the butt of the Colt for which he was reaching and he went down in a sprawling heap.

Although Wallace too had commenced his draw, before he could even touch the glossy white handle, he learned that there was a serious disadvantage to carrying the short barrelled Colt in such a fashion. As soon as she had struck the man behind her, relying upon Turner to protect her from the other hard-case, Madam Bulldog thrust forward her right hand and beat the gambler to grasping the butt of his weapon. A tug brought it from the cross draw holster and she spun swiftly upon her heel. Just as the man she had struck was coming to a halt and preparing to resume his efforts, he once again found himself circumvented.

'I can copper that bet, too!' the blonde warned, thumb cocking the revolver.

Finding he was suddenly looking into the muzzle of the Colt, which seemed far larger than its .36 calibre under the circumstances, the hard-case froze the movement of his right hand well clear of his weapon. Every instinct warned him that the new owner of the Hide And Horn Saloon was far from being inexperienced at handling a revolver. Nor did he doubt she would 'copper that bet, too', although much more dangerously than when the term was employed in the game of faro, if he tried to take further action against her.

Stumbling backwards a few steps in fright, as he felt himself being relieved of his weapon, Wallace halted beyond the reach of the saloon's new owner. While he would have been willing enough to have drawn and used the Colt if granted an opportunity, undeterred by his intended victim being a woman, he was far from courageous. Therefore, despite her back being to him, he had no intention of tackling her personally until he had satisfied himself with regards to how much support he could count upon from elsewhere in the bar-room.

Looking around, the gambler discovered there would be little or no help available. He concluded his lucrative occupancy of the premises was to be suspended, or—unless his half-sister could find a legal loophole in their favour—permanently ended.

At the far table, the Fletcher brothers were starting to rise. Guessing there was something more than an accident behind the wrecking of the box and the insistence that it should be replaced by a different kind, a supposition increased by seeing Madam presenting it to Wallace, the players realised there was more to the new owner than they had at first thought. Deciding that discretion was the better part of valour, the dealer and the case-keeper sank back on to their chairs.

Not far away, another gambler was standing up. As he was about to leave the table, he found himself confronted by the five cowhands from the Leaning J ranch. They were no longer looking amiable and he too concluded it would be advisable to mind his own business.

Yet a fourth gambler quit his seat. As he was starting to cross the room, he was tripped by Viola Grant. A fifth had a tray of drinks tipped into his lap by a waiter as he was coming to his feet. At the wheel of fortune, the operator changed his intentions on being eyed malevolently by the two elderly swampers. Although neither Joshua Gilmore nor his cronies were showing signs of being prepared to intervene, the dealer at the *vingt-un* table also elected to remain passive. Nor were the remainder of the men brought to Tennyson by Wallace willing, or able, to intercede in the face of the open hostility displayed towards them by various other members of the saloon's work force.

'Go and stand by your boss!' Madam ordered the bodyguard she was covering. Without allowing the revolver to waver, she contrived to gaze about her and was delighted to discover she had won over so many of her employees, and some customers. 'Move it!'

'S—Sure!' Lang replied and obeyed with alacrity.

'Well, now, Mr. Wallace,' the blonde said, turning to direct a cold gaze upon the gambler. 'Happen you don't reckon I can handle this hogleg any better than I can play poker?'

Concluding the question, Madam dipped and fired the Colt in a rapid motion. Splinters erupted from the floor just in front of the gambler's right boot, causing him to make an involuntary bound away. As soon as he landed, the alignment of the short barrel having been altered, a second bullet was sent equally close to his other foot. Twice more, on alighting from a frightened leap, he was induced to take off again by lead splattering his feet with more slivers of wood.

'*Satisfied*?' Madam challenged, lifting the smoking weapon until its muzzle was directed at the centre of Wallace's narrow chest.

'Y—Yes!' the gambler confirmed, his sallow face even paler. The quivering was no longer rage, but terror.

'And you're just as satisfied I'm telling the truth about winning this place from Maxie fair and square?' the blonde damanded.

'S—Sure you did!' Wallace conceded, staring as if mesmerised at his own Colt.

'I'm right pleased to hear it,' Madam said dryly. 'Well now, I don't know what kind of deal your sister made Maxie give you, but I'll honour it—providing you can prove to Counselor Scrope's satisfaction that it's still *legally* binding now I own the place. There's only one thing, though.'

'What's that?' Wallace asked sullenly and without hope, remembering the document he was given by his half-sister stated his control of the gambling only lasted while Maxwell Higgins was owner of the saloon.

'That Marshal Collier and I go over *every* piece of gambling equipment together,' the blonde explained, lowering the Colt and deftly flicking the percussion caps from the two chambers of the cylinder which were still loaded. 'Happen we find they're all right, you can go on running things.'

'I'll have all my gear moved out comes morning!' the gambler stated, being all to aware of what the result of the examination by the clearly knowledgeable woman would be. 'Come on, Herb!'

'Take your other bully-boy with you,' Madam ordered, indicating the hard-case felled by Turner. Then, tossing the Colt to its owner, her right hand whisked under the jacket of her travelling costume. Before he had caught the weapon, it reappeared grasping the butt of a British made Webley Bulldog revolver which had been in a carefully designed shoulder holster she was wearing.[3] Not needing to cock the hammer manually, the mechanism being 'double action', she pointed the stubby barrel at him and continued, 'Here, I'm toting my own and can shoot even better with it.'

'Looks like we ain't going to be needed after all, Tune,' commented Deputy Town Marshal Herman 'Pockets' Hoscroft, from where he and his superior were standing just beyond the batwing doors of the front entrance to the saloon.

'Looks like it,' Town Marshal Tune Collier agreed, having considered it advisable to be close by on hearing Wallace had returned earlier than anticpated from the county seat. He had been correct in his assumption that the new owner would be unwilling to go along with the arrangement he believed had been forced upon her predecessor. Furthermore, it seemed—even though he had failed to catch those responsible—his suspicion that there were dishonest methods being employed in some, if not all, the games was correct. Feeling certain the situation would be changed for the better, he ran his gaze appreciatively over the attractive and competent blonde, continuing, 'She's quite a woman, Pockets!'

'You've just said a Texas sized mouthful, *amigo*,'

3. *Regardless of the name given to the weapon used by Madam Bulldog even in the revised information we have received, as the 'British Bulldog' Model was not manufactured by the company until around 1878, there is a distinct possibility it was actually a modified Webley Royal Irish Constabulary revolver. The misconception could have been caused by an erroneous belief that the selection of firearm had created her sobriquet. However, in case we are mistaken and, furthermore, to avoid confusion as we supplied the designation 'Webley Bulldog' to her revolver in,* CUT ONE, THEY ALL BLEED, *we will continue to refer to it by that name in this volume. J.T.E.*

enthused the deputy. 'One way and another, I reckon she's going to make a whole heap of changes in that ole saloon.'

'And in the town, likely,' Collier assessed. 'Come on. Let's back off a ways. I want to have a few words with Wallace when he comes out to let him know how things stand.'

While withdrawing, neither peace officer envisaged just what an effect upon their lives and the town of Tennyson as a whole the woman calling herself 'Madam Bulldog' was going to have!

CHAPTER EIGHT

I'll Blow Your God-damned Head Off

'Well now, gents, I'm obliged for you having stayed over so's we can talk things out,' Madam Bulldog asserted, lounging comfortably against the mahogany counter as if she had done the same for years. Looking from one to another of the ten operators of the gambling games assembled for her by Joseph Turner, she continued in the same amiable tone, 'I know you were all brought here by Leo Wallace and, although I *might* be doing you an injustice, I reckon I've a pretty fair notion why you were picked. That's none of my never-mind. He's gone and he *won't* be coming back.'

The buxom and attractive blonde looked completely relaxed, at peace with the world and satisfied by her lot in life!

Nor, although she still had a matter of considerable importance demanding her attention, was the appearance presented by the new owner of the Hide And Horn Saloon misleading!

To Madam's way of thinking, (a point of view shared by her newly appointed floor manager and the majority of her employees) her first night in control had been an unqualified success. Business had been brisk and profitable. Furthermore, after she had dealt so competently with the threat posed by Wallace and his bodyguards, there was no further trouble. A visit later by Town Marshal Tune Collier and his deputy had not been in the line of duty, and the advice he had given to the deposed head of gambling was never mentioned. Instead, he and Deputy Marshal Herman 'Pockets' Hoscroft had drunk to the health and continued success of the new owner before resuming their briefly interrupted rounds.

Joshua Gilmore had subjected the blonde to what he clearly believed to be irresistible charm which, presumably, he had used with considerable success upon other members of her sex. Far from being impressed, although she had behaved in a friendly fashion, she had excused herself from his company on the grounds that she needed to circulate and get to know the other customers. Despite the blacksmith having made no attempt to conceal displeasure over what was tantamount to a dismissal (which had seemed to amuse his cronies on that account) they had all behaved themselves for the rest of the evening.

Madam had established a far more satisfactory relationship with another group of local businessmen. One, moreover, of greater prominence and influence— should they care to exert it—than Gilmore and his companions. Joining Lawyer Aloysius P. Scrope, she had been introduced formally to the party he had brought to make her acquainatance. Such had been the skill with which she had handled them that, far from being annoyed at her delay in reaching their table, they had considered it a tribute to their importance that she had given attention to 'lesser' customers first and was now willing to spend the rest of the evening in their company.

Showing an intelligent appreciation of the situation with regard to the most recent developments in the state of affairs at Austin, the blonde had done much to relieve their concern over how her presence might affect the chances of Tennyson supplanting Garnett as seat of Sand County. She had made an appointment to visit Gavin Standish, owner of the Cattlemen's Bank— apologising for talking business at such a moment—in

92

the morning to make a substantial deposit of cash. Others of the group, including the manager of the Fortescue Hotel and short, peppery Doctor Henry Connel—the only medical practitioner in the area— had gone away satisfied by the indications of the possible business advantages which were likely to accrue from her ownership of the Hide And Horn Saloon.

Taking into account the generally pleasant atmosphere all evening and the way several of the customers had said their good nights on leaving, Madam felt she had made as good an impression upon them as with the party accompanying the attorney. Now, with Young 'N' closing the front entrance to signify business was concluded for the day, and other employees starting to tidy up, she was setting about a matter of some importance.

Of various heights, builds, hair colours and ages, between the mid twenties and late fifties, not one of the men to whom the blonde was speaking wore the traditional attire of professional gamblers. Instead, their town style clothing gave no indication of how they might earn their living. That every one of them, with the exception of the Fletcher brothers, wore a firearm of some kind visible upon his person was not unusual. In most places west of the Mississippi River, a man without a gun was the exception rather than the rule.

'He won't, huh?' grunted the burly and black haired gambler over whom the waiter, Sam, had spilled the drinks during the confrontation with Wallace. 'Then how's that leave *us*?'

'In what way?' Madam inquired, although she had a good idea of what the answer was going to be.

'What about our *pay*?'

'Are you owed any?'

'Yeah!'

'Then, was I you, I'd take it up with *him*,' the blonde advised. 'I reckon you know where you can find him.

93

At least, I hope you do. Because he *won't* be coming in here again!'

'Is that what you've got us here to tell us?' growled the lanky and heavily moustached man who had backed down from the threat displayed by the five cowhands.

'No, but it was brought up and I reckoned you might as well know how I stand,' Madam replied, and her manner indicated she would brook no argument on the subject. 'What I've had you come over here for is Joe Turner reckons you're all good at running your games. He's floor boss now, and I'm willing to take his word on it.'

'*Floor boss?*' sniggered the middle-sized and over weight dealer for the *vingt-un* table. He belonged to the 'sporting' crowd led by Gilmore and had heard the comments made about the blonde's possible morals. Swinging a mocking gaze towards the man in question, he went on in tones of derision, 'And you a *married* man, for sh——!'

Stepping forward swiftly, before Turner could register a similar objection to the completely undeserved comment, the blonde brought it to an abrupt end by knotting and whipping up her left fist. Struck under the side of his jaw by the powerful and skilfully delivered blow, the gambler was knocked in a twirling sprawl from amongst his companions. He was brought to a halt by the sturdy table over which he had been presiding. Accepting his weight, without collapsing or turning over, it prevented him from falling to the floor. Nevertheless, he slid from it to land in a keeling posture. Snarling a profanity, he reached towards the butt of the revolver tucked beneath the dark blue silk sash around his bulging and far from solid midsection. Effective as such a means of carrying the weapon had proved in the past, he was somewhat dazed by the unexpected and surprisingly hard blow and fumbled instead of making a smooth draw.

'Leave it be!' Madam commanded, bringing out her

Webley Bulldog revolver with a speed similar to that employed when dealing with Wallace earlier in the evening. This time, however, she drew back the hammer with her thumb even though the 'double action' mechanism did not require this to be done before it could operate. With her left hand joining the right on the 'bird's head' style, ivory gripped butt, she elevated the two and a half inch barrel of the weapon until at arms' length and shoulder height, permitting a more accurate aim to be taken. 'If that hog-leg comes clear of the sash, I'll blow your god-damned head off!'

Despite the dizziness which was swirling inside his throbbing skull, the gambler could hear and understand what was being said. Furthermore, staring through eyes partially dazzled by what appeared to be brightly flashing lights, he realized he could be in deadly danger. He did not doubt the woman he had insulted meant and was fully capable of doing what she had threatened. There was not the slightest wavering in the heavy calibre, British-made weapon, nor any suggestion on the part of its owner that there would be any hesitation before using it. Shaking his head, in an attempt to clear it, he snatched his hand well clear of the revolver it had just touched. Then he struggled erect with the aid of the table. Using this for support, due to the wobbly condition of his legs, he waited with anxiety to find out what was in store for him next.

'I thought you'd see things *my* way!' Madam stated, returning the Webley to its shoulder holster. Swinging her gaze around the other gamblers, she challenged, 'Has anybody else got anything to say on those lines?'

'It shouldn't've been said in the first place, ma'am,' Abel Fletcher asserted. Having been told by Turner of the decision reached with regards to himself and his twin brother, he had no desire for their future to be jeopardized. 'Which, I reckon Matt McDonald there's wishing he hadn't been so smart-assed and said it.'

'I reckon you could just about be right at that,' the blonde declared.

'What did you have in mind for us house-men, ma'am?' Cain Fletcher inquired, sharing the sentiments of his sibling and wanting to show his gratitude by bringing about a resumption of the conversation which had been interrupted.

'I thought *nobody* was going to ask,' Madam answered. 'But, seeing's somebody did, I'm willing to keep on any of you who've a mind to stay.'

'Doing what we done for Leo Wallace?' asked the tall and skinny operator of the Wheel Of Fortune, being the oldest of the group.

'*No!*' the blonde corrected emphatically. 'Strange as it might make some of you reckon I am, I'll expect you to play *fair* and we'll let the house's percentages take care of making the profits.'

'You saying we ain't been playing *fair?*' growled the gambler who had posed the first question, without any real justification.

'I don't give a damn whether you have or haven't,' Madam claimed, showing no sign of being disturbed by the hostile glare to which she was being subjected. 'I'm only telling you how it's going to be from now on.'

'I reckon Brother Cain 'n' me're willing to go along with that, ma'am!' Abel announced, never having been comfortable while following the orders received from Wallace and employing dishonest methods. 'We've thought some on it and conclude you was right about which kind of dealer box's *best* to use.'

'Which being, we're wanting to stay on, ma'am,' Cain supported his sibling. 'Happen you'll have us, that is.'

'Then, damned if I don't give it a whirl with you,' Madam accepted and stated how much she was willing to pay to any of the group who elected to remain in her employment. Sensing that all of them considered it better than they had been receiving from Wallace, she went on without asking who was willing to stay, 'There's something else, though. Sam, will you and Sonny fetch down the big black trunk from my rooms, please?'

'Sure thing, ma'am,' the waiter replied and crossed the bar-room accompanied by the second of the elderly swampers. On their return, they were carrying the requested bulky item from the baggage which had been sent to the saloon that afternoon by the agent of the Wells Fargo depot. 'Is this the one you're wanting?'

'That's the one,' the blonde confirmed, having spent the collection time being introduced to, and learning something about, each of the gamblers. Unlocking the trunk with a key on the small bunch she took from the pocket of her jacket, she reached inside and announced, 'Unless it makes some of you change your mind about staying on, this's what I'll expect you to wear while you're running your games.'

After looking at the items removed from the trunk by the woman, the gamblers exchanged glances. Shaking out the folded black shirt and trousers, she held them up after the fashion of an assistant in a big city store specializing in masculine attire. Displaying the garments for a few seconds, while her gaze passed from one to another of them, she brought it to a halt upon the tall, well built and youngest of the group, whose name she had learned was Charles Henderson.

'Yes,' Madam said, nodding in approval. 'I reckon we've got your fit without needing too many alterations, Charlie.'

'Why'd they need to fit?' queried Jabez Wilmott, the man who had been subjected to the intervention of the cowhands.

'*All* the fellers working the games will be dressed in these kind of shirts and pants,' the blonde explained. 'But I'll leave what kind of boots you have on to you.'

'Does the same apply to hats, ma'am?' inquired Cain Fletcher, bare headed as was his brother.

'No *gentleman* would wear his hat indoors, for shame,' Madam pointed out, matching the amiability

97

with which the question had been posed. 'And I aim to have well dressed *gentlemen* handling the tables.'

'What's wrong with our own clothes?' asked the burly and black haired gambler, Otis Chiffoner, looking downwards at his somewhat stained attire.

'Nothing, for *outside*,' the blonde admitted, then she indicated the marks caused by the drinks which had been spilled by the waiter. 'In here, wearing my gear, happen you have another *accident* like that, you can easy enough go change in the backroom I'll have set out for you and it'll be the house who has to pay to get them cleaned.'

'Hey!' Henderson put in, having stepped forward to take and examine the garments. They were well made from good quality and durable material. Being a snappy dresser, he approved of the double breasted cut of the shirt. However, on examining the trousers, he noticed they differed in one aspect from any others he had seen. 'There's only this one lil pocket in the pants!'

'I *know*,' Madam admitted. 'For one thing, Izzy Cohen, the tailor up to Cowtown, said it would save him, and everybody else he could get to handle a needle and stitching thread, time to make them that way. Which, I didn't leave him a whole heap of time to get enough made ready to give me a start here.'

'That's as maybe!' Matthew McDonald mumbled, speaking slowly to reduce the throbbing in his bruised jaw. Like all the others in the group, he was aware that there was another reason for the insistence on wearing the exhibited attire, the lack of pockets in the trousers and being bare headed. 'Only there's some's might reckon you're as good's saying you don't *trust* us!'

'Perish the thought!' the blonde asserted, with such a disarming smile she might have been sincere in the protestation. 'Whoever heard of a house man who wasn't to be *trusted*?'

'Then why the fancy duds, ma'am?' asked Barney Clifton, the operator of the Wheel Of Fortune, but his tone was more friendly than when he had previously spoken.

'Could be so the bouncers will be able to pick you out from the customers and won't whomp you by mistake in a ruckus,' Madam suggested.

'Now that's something I'm all for!' Abel Fletcher claimed. 'Moe Stern near on hit me one time when there was fuss with some of the cowhands and I don't even dress like they do.'

'That doesn't surprise me, what I saw of him,' the blonde declared. 'And, speaking of Moe Stern, he won't be coming back again either.'

'I heard he got something in his belly that didn't agree with him, ma'am,' Henderson put in, eyeing his new employer with frank admiration.

'Or he didn't agree with,' Chiffoner supplemented, also having been told of how the blonde had dealt with the former head bouncer. He realized that, in addition to her ability to defend herself, she was also shrewd and well versed in the problems of running the gambling activities of a saloon. Reaching a decision, he went on, 'Would you have a shirt and pants that'll fit me, ma'am?'

'There should be,' Madam replied. 'At least, close enough until Saul Bernstein can take measurements and make up a good fit.'

'How about for Brother Abel and me?' the second Fletcher twin asked.

'You can try for some comes morning,' the blonde promised.

'By golly, ma'am,' Wilmott commented, also with greater amiability. 'We'll look as fancy as the house men at the Silver Bell in Cowtown!'

'And a heap more handsome, Jabez,' Madam answered, having noticed the use of the word, 'we'; she did not mention that it was she who had suggested the wearing of such attire by the gambling crew to the owner of the Silver Bell in the first place.

Nor did the blonde intend, at that time, to say anything about her intention of matching something else for which the Silver Bell Saloon in Fort Worth was famous!

CHAPTER NINE

I'll Get Back That Saloon

'Well, god damn it, I'll say one thing!' Wanda Higgins spat out furiously, her voice, which was sometimes sultry and enticing, holding no suggestion of its usual seductive promise. Looking with undisguised loathing from her half-brother to her brother and back, as they stood sheepishly before her in the expensively furnished sitting-room of her home, she continued just as harshly, 'You pair certainly showed just what you're worth yesterday, going by what you've just told me!'

Five foot seven in her bare feet, which she was at that moment, the wife of the Hide And Horn Saloon's previous owner had only recently passed her thirtieth birthday. Generally elegant and glamorous, albeit in a way which was indicative of her former occupation as an entertainer in the middle echelons of the theatrical profession, she was far from looking at her best at that moment. Her normally stylishly coiffured henna red hair was dishevelled, and the make up on her arrogantly beautiful face, invariably far more extensive than was considered socially acceptable for a 'good' woman, was badly in need of renovation. She had a full bosomed Junoesque figure which was remarkably firm—in view of her generally slothful and self indulgent way of life—and still nearly as well muscled as when she had been noted as an exceptionally active and vigorous dancer on the stage. The robe she had draped over an almost transparent black silk nightgown and left unfastened did little to conceal her eye-catching contours.

Never at its best in the early morning, or even close to noon—the time she usually left her bed—Wanda's temper was far from improved by the unwonted activity which had been thrust upon her the previous afternoon, and by having been compelled to rise long before her usual hour. Looking forward to a more extensive dalliance in Garnett, improving her far from platonic relationship with County Sheriff Lloyd Bowman and indulging in some instruction of a special nature he had arranged for her, the telegraph message sent by the gambler to inform her of the situation at home had caused her to return to Tennyson in considerable haste.

On arriving at her home late the previous night, and finding neither Wallace—whose relationship stemmed only from her father having married a widow with a son after the death of her mother—nor Moses Stern present, the red head had gone to bed in no amiable frame of mind. Having slept indifferently and been woken much earlier than she would have preferred, her mood had grown increasingly malevolent on hearing the information they had to impart when they put in an appearance, and the disdain she felt, particularly for her hulking full brother, was becoming more apparent by the minute.

'Aw hell, Wan'!' Stern mumbled, feeling gingerly at his still aching stomach. He had missed inheriting both the good looks and the intelligence of his sister. 'She hit me when I wasn't looking!'

'She'd probably have found it even easier if you had been looking!' Wanda snorted and changed the baleful glare to her half-brother. 'And I suppose *you* wasn't looking when she took your god-damned gun away from you?'

'I was trying to find out what'd happened to Barry

Norman,' Wallace excused himself sullenly and with no greater veracity than had been displayed by the former head bouncer. Somewhat less in awe of the arrogantly beautiful woman, he went on irritably, 'Who the hell could've figured she'd grab my gun?'

'Not *you*, obviously!' Wanda hissed, clenching her fists in anger. 'And those two god damned hard-cases you've been spending *my* money on didn't show to any great shakes as bodyguards!'

'They got took by surprise—!' the gambler began, keeping a wary eye on the red head's knotted hands as he was well aware of her proclivity to use them impartially when her temper was aroused.

'For the "mother-something" money they've been getting, I wouldn't have expected them to get *"took by surprise"*!' Wanda answered, practically spitting out the last three words. 'Or taken any other god damed way, comes to that. And I suppose all those over paid tinhorns *you* insisted on bringing in "got took by surprise" like you three?'

'Joe Turner and just about every other son-of-a-bitch in the place took cards to stop them cutting in,' Wallace asserted, with somewhat more truth than previously. 'And that includes Maxie's girl, Vi Grant.'

'I'd expect some god damned grandstand play from *her*, the stinking, tail peddling calico cat!' the red head claimed viciously and thought with satisfaction of certain preparations she had been making to deal with the woman she had heard was on intimate terms with her husband. Driving her right fist into the palm of the left hand she had opened with a solid 'thwack!', she went on, 'Just wait until I get her down to the Barnhof and in Rudy Schanz's r——!'

'What I've heard,' the gambler interrupted, although he found the proposal to which his half sister was referring not without interest. 'It's lucky they got stopped.'

'Why?'

'From all accounts, seems like this Madam Bulldog's

103

got Tune Collier licking her feet same as Lawyer Scrope.'

'God damn it!' Wanda snapped, reaching with a jewelled hand to run its fingers through the dishevelled hair. 'She didn't waste any time!'

'Not a god damned minute, was I asked,' Wallace confirmed. However, with his half-sister in her present mood, he considered he would be ill-advised to mention she had failed to achieve anything like a similar friendship with either the peace officer or the attorney, despite having tried for a longer period than Madam Bulldog had been in Tennyson. 'And not only with them two!'

'How do you mean?' the red head demanded.

'She'd even got Josh Gilmore and his bunch ready to back her,' the gambler lied, unable to resist the temptation of supplying incorrect information which he knew would annoy the arrogant beauty. Seeing the savage glint which came into her eyes at the suggestion that one of her conquests had seemingly transferred his affections, he went on hurriedly, 'Which being, the last thing I wanted was a ruckus between them and our house men.'

'Why not?' Wanda challenged. 'It wouldn't have done this *Madam Bulldog* any good with the stuffed shirts around this god-damned one horse town to have a roughhouse brawl in the saloon the first night she took over.'

'It wouldn't have done *us* any good, either,' Wallace warned. 'Fact being, we'd likely have come out of it worse than her.'

'How come?'

'She'd busted up what she'd knowed was a second dealer box and, seeing's how the game was still going on, she must've guessed about the drawer, and she made the Fletcher boys play with a straight 'n' and a deck of clean cards from out of it. So the last thing I wanted was for Collier brought in by a ruckus.'

'It wouldn't have been all that *bad* for us,' Wanda

estimated. 'What with the table having showed up and put in so soon before she arrived, there's plenty who'd have thought it was her who'd sent it.'

'No they wouldn't, or at least they'd soon've learned they was wrong,' the gambler contradicted, looking even more ill at ease as he realized his confession was unlikely to improve the bad temper shown by the red head. 'She'd already suckered me into admitting it was *our* table. With that known, seeing Collier let me know how things stood 'twixt him and her when I came out, it'd've gone bad for *us* happen he'd got showed a secret drawer with the other second dealers and some decks of readers[1] in it on *our* faro table.'

'Do you reckon she was telling the truth about how she got the Hide from that no account husband of mine?' Wanda inquired, holding her temper in check with an effort as she noticed the emphasis placed upon the words, '*us*' and '*our*'. She deduced correctly, that her half-brother would not have absolved her of complicity if he had been arrested for operating the cheating devices. 'Hell, I know he was a lousy poker player, but I'd've thought he'd know enough to quit before he got in that *deep*!'

'Scrope and Collier don't reckon he did,' Wallace pointed out. 'Which's what counts!'

'Like hell it is!' the red head denied heatedly. 'All right, so it might *here*, but it won't down to the county seat.'

'If he didn't lose it to her,' Stern put in, striving with his limited intelligence and imagination to keep track of the conversation. 'How come she's here telling everybody's he did?'

'He'd send her here with fake papers, making out she'd won it from him in the Big One,' the red head explained, with a blatant patience which a person of greater perception would have found more annoying

---

1. '*Readers*': gamblers' term for marked cards. J.T.E.

than openly displayed irritation or animosity. 'That's how!'

'Why'd he do that?' the hulking man pursued, showing a complete lack of comprehension.

'It could be he's hoping that,' Wanda continued, starting to grit out the words in growing exasperation, 'we'd get the hell out of his life, thinking he'd lost the saloon and there'd be no more money coming in.'

'Yeah!' Stern admitted, the idea having failed to occur to him before. He continued, in a tone redolent of self righteous indignation, 'The bastard's slick enough to've pulled a play like that. And mean enough, comes to that!'

'Aw hell, Wan!' Wallace commented, despite knowing Maxwell Higgins had been given adequate cause for any 'meanness' he might be slick enough to indulge in where his wife and her dependant relatives were concerned. 'If that's what's behind it, all we have to do is say so and get her throwed out on her fat fanny!'

'I didn't say that's what's behind it, all I said was "if" it had happened,' the red head said. Rising from the table at which she had seated herself, although she had not offered either man a chair and they knew better than to sit down without being invited, she went on, 'And even *if* that should be what his game is, Scrope and probably Collier will be in cahoots with him. So we're going to have to *prove* what's happened, whether it really did, or we just reckon it was pulled that way.'

'How the hell are we going to do *that*?' the gambler asked. 'Particularly if she did win it fair and square.'

'How the "something" do I know how we'll do the "mother-something", whether we're right or wrong?' the red head snapped, her language growing more profane as was always the case in moments of stress or excitement. It was a trait which had done much to make her extremely unpopular with the 'good' women of the town; this being an age long before the employment of such terms by members of her sex was

106

accepted as a 'trendy' indication of sterling 'liberal' qualities. A pensive expression came to her face and, as was also always the case when wanting to give thought to a serious problem, she began to pace the room in a sensuous glide which drew a lascivious gaze from her half-brother; even Stern watched her with less than filial attention. Coming to a halt and showing no sign of being perturbed by their faces she announced, 'I'd best see that skinny gutted jury fixer and find out exactly how the land lies.'

'Yeah, that'd be best!' seconded the hulking man, tearing his gaze from the pulsating and skimpily covered breasts which his sister was deliberately causing to jut forward over her trim and firm stomach. Then, as her cold gaze turned his way, he started to shuffle his feet. He felt, as was frequently the case when in her company, like a dim witted schoolboy. 'So what do you want us to do while you're at it, Wan'?'

'You can come and help me get our gear out of the Hide And Horn,' Wallace stated, also wrenching his lecherous eyes from the red head and giving her no chance to reply. The words sounded more in the nature of an order to an underling than a request made to a member of the family.

'Why the "something" should you move it out?' Wanda demanded, pausing as she was about to make her way to the stairs.

'She reckoned's how she was aiming to look it all over with Collier,' the gambler replied. 'So we'd best get it out afore they can.'

'Leave the bastard where it is!' the red head commanded, her manner similar to that employed by Wallace when addressing her brother. 'I'll get back the saloon if it's the last thing I do, and having all the crooked gear left in it just might help.'

'How?' the gambler challenged, thinking of the cost of the equipment which he had partly borne when making the purchase at the instigation of his half-sister.

107

'I've got *something* in mind, don't worry!' Wanda replied, with what appeared to be complete confidence, although at that moment she had only the bare nucleus of a scheme. 'So you just leave it where it is until I tell you different. Right now, I'm going to get dressed and go find out all I can from Scrope. You head 'round there and let him know to expect me at eleven, Moe.'

'Sure, Wan'!' Stern assented.

'I'll come with y—!' Wallace began.

'The hell you will!' the red head corrected. 'You stay here and out of sight. I'm going to spread the word that you've left town. Moe, after you've seen Scrope, find Norman and Lang and tell them not to show themselves until I've talked to them.'

'How long do I stay here?' the gambler asked sullenly, as the hulking man nodded concurrence with the the latest order.

'Until I tell you differently!' Wanda replied and swung on her heel to make for the staircase without allowing any further discussion on the matter. However, pausing at the foot, she looked around and went on, 'Tell Scrope to have that "Madam Bulldog" woman there as well, Moe!'

'You figuring on taking her 'stead of Vi Grant, Wan'?' Stern inquired.

'It could maybe come to that,' the red head admitted grimly. 'But I want to look her over first and see what kind of opposition I figure she might be.'

* * *

'Hell, boss, I'm *sorry*!' Viola Grant apologised, stepping hurriedly from the second floor balcony and, as if considering there was an urgent need for ensuring privacy although there was nobody else on it, closing the door of the room she entered. 'I din't even know you was out of the sack yet, much less guess what I'd find you doing up here!'

The time was quarter after ten in the morning, and there was justification for the latter part of the statement by the boss girl!

Due to the sturdy way in which the Hide And Horn Saloon was constructed, there had been no indication downstairs of the activity being carried out by the new owner. It had been the habit of Maxwell Higgins to sleep until almost noon on the numerous occasions when he elected to remain in the saloon instead of going home, and the brunette had heard nothing to suggest her new boss would behave in a different fashion. Certainly there had been nothing to indicate how Madam Bulldog was engaged in the main bedroom of what was now her personal living accommodation. Nor, if asked, would Viola even have thought of finding her occupied in such a manner; particularly after the strenuous activities of the previous day.

Wearing only a pair of black cotton tights, such as were used during rehearsals or training by ballet and other kinds of dancers, the blonde was lying with only her head and shoulders on the carpet covered floor. Having elevated her curvaceous buttocks to almost vertical, she was moving her sturdy legs through the air in a circular motion similar to that of a person riding and operating the peddles of one of the 'boneshaker' bicycles which were becoming popular in the cities of the East.

'That's all right, Vi,' Madam replied amiably, bringing her feet down and up to with an agility and ease which might have appeared surprising considering her less than slender build. 'I should have thought to tell you I always do some exercises dressed like this in the morning, straight after I get out of the sack. The other gear I sometimes use will be coming along with my other stuff on a freight wagon in the next day or so.'

With that, the blonde spread her legs apart and placed hands on hips. Bending forward at the waist, she began to vigorously rotate her torso. Watching her, the brunette was able to form an even better impres-

109

sion of how she had been able to deliver such a powerful punch. There was not an ounce of flabby fat anywhere on her shapely buxom figure. Instead, well developed and clearly firm muscles writhed and pulsated beneath her smooth skin. Their fluid and seemingly effortless movements provided testimony to the strength, backed by speed and agility, which they were capable of exerting.

'Whooee!' the boss girl gasped in admiration, as her employer straightened up. 'You do this sort of thing *every* morning?'

'I try not to miss doing it, or something just as lively,' Madam answered with a grin, contriving to speak almost normally in spite of her massive and firm bosom expanding and contracting as proof of the effort she had been putting into the exercises. Extending her arms forward at shoulder height, but keeping her back straight, she began to bend her knees until her thighs were parallel to the floor. Returning slowly to an erect posture, she repeated the squatting motion while continuing in a slightly more breathless fashion, 'It keeps me in shape for handling awkward cusses who rile me. Anyways, what's brought you up here?'

'Lawyer Scrope's just sent around word's he'd like to see you in his office at eleven,' Viola explained, showing no resentment over the comment, despite having qualifed as one of the 'awkward cusses' during her first meeting with the blonde.

'I was aiming to drop by some time this morning, anyways,' Madam admitted, having completed fifteen of the exercises to improve the strength of the back. 'But have you any idea why he wants me to go there right then?'

'Seems like that red haired bitch's married Max— Mrs. Higgins sent him word's she wants to talk to you and him,' the boss girl replied, making a face which demonstrated her feelings where the wife of the former owner was concerned. 'He said he figured you'd want to be on hand to hear what she's got in mind.'

'He's right as the Indian side of a horse,' the blonde confirmed. 'I didn't know Maxie was married when I won the Hide And Horn from him, so I reckon I'd best look her over and see whether I reckon she's got a raw deal out of him.'

'The only thing she ever got that was raw'd be the inside of her thighs when she was lying on her back in bed,' Viola claimed. 'And that *wouldn't* have been caused by *Maxie*!'

'I'll keep an open mind on it,' Madam declared, knowing her image would be improved in the town if she treated the wife of the man she had supplanted with fairness, even if this was undeserved. 'Can you get some water here, so's I can wash and get ready to go and meet her?'

CHAPTER TEN

If I Wasn't A *Lady*

'Good morning to you, Madam Bulldog!' Aloysius P. Scrope greeted, rising from behind his desk, as the new owner of the Hide And Horn Saloon was shown into his office some five minutes before the time he had requested her attendance. Indicating the two chairs placed at the other side, as his daughter withdrew and closed the connecting door, he went on, 'Take a seat, please. I'm afraid Mrs. Higgins isn't here yet.'

'I'd sort of got a notion she *wasn't*,' the blonde claimed with a warm smile, thinking the appearance and dour behaviour of the attorney was so similar to her last visit that he might never have left his desk. Sitting on the chair furthest away from the door through which she had been admitted, she went on, 'Seems likely she doesn't know Sergeant Paddy Magoon, pride of the United States' Cavalry.'[1]

1. *Some information regarding the career of Sergeant Seamus Patrick 'Paddy' Magoon, United States' Cavalry, can be found in:* THE RUSHERS, APACHE RAMPAGE *and, by inference,* HELL IN THE PALO DURO, GO BACK TO HELL *and* THE SOUTH WILL RISE AGAIN. *However, when recording in* TROUBLE TRAIL *a meeting he had with a very close relation of Madam Bulldog, Miss Martha 'Calamity Jane' Canary, due to an error in the source from which we were producing the manuscript, we referred to him as 'Sergeant Paddy Muldoon'. As yet, we have not*

112

'If he wears trousers, which his rank and name presupposes would prove the case, I'd be much surprised if she *didn't* know him,' Scrope asserted dryly and, apparently, with complete seriousness. 'But I fail to see why her absence should lead you to assume she has not made his acquaintance.'

'Paddy always reckons a good soldier gets on parade five minutes early,' Madam explained, with a similar suggestion of imparting solemn and vitally important information. Then, although there was little discernible change in her manner, the levity left her and she went on, 'Anyways, I hope Mrs. Higgins doesn't decide to exercise a woman's prerogative and show up too late so as to impress us. There're a whole heap of things I want to get done before we open up the Hide this afternoon.'

On hearing that her presence had been requested by the attorney, the blonde had wasted no time in making ready for the visit. Stripping off the tights, she had washed the perspiration from her buxom body with water delivered to the smaller bedroom of her living accommodation by the swampers, Sonny and Young 'N'. Then, having tidied her hair and applied the socially acceptable amount of facial make up, she had donned clean clothing of a similarly respectable style to those worn the previous day. Normally a hearty eater, one reason for her vigorous session of exercises every possible morning, she had restricted her breakfast to a cup of coffee brought upstairs by Viola Grant. By doing so, wanting to speak privately with Scrope and sure Wanda Higgins would not show an equal punctuality, she had contrived to keep the appointment earlier than was stipulated.

'Did you have a good first night?' the attorney inquired.

'It had its *moments*,' Madam replied cheerfully. 'But,

---

been able to discover where Madam met Magoon, or what happened.
J.T.E.

taken all in all, I don't reckon I got too bad a deal out of Maxie.'

'One might even go so far as to say you've got a *good* deal,' the attorney corrected, with professional caution.

'Only "*might even*"?' Madam challenged with a smile. 'And here's poor lil ole me thinking I had got one!'

'Let us say there is a *reasonable* probability you did, if you would rather,' Scrope suggested, his face as apparently unemotional as the aged parchment which his skin resembled, but there was a twinkle in his eye belying the sombre manner. 'As I mentioned yesterday, Joe Turner and I have been handling the day to day business and operation of the saloon, in the absence of Maxwell Higgins. Even the gambling side, until the arrival of Leo Wallace and his minions.'

'I thought Mrs. Higgins had been running things?' Madam commented, resisting the temptation to adopt a similar style of dry speech to that of the attorney.

'A not unnatural assumption,' Scrope conceded. 'However, apart from finding employment for her indigent kin, Mrs. Wanda Higgins was only interested in getting all the money she needed from the profits, not in how they were accrued.'

'I'm beginning not to like Mrs. Wanda Higgins!' the blonde claimed.

'Then you share the sentiments of practically every other member of your gender in Tennyson,' the attorney asserted, but he was doing something more than merely passing the time in idle gossip. Although he had acted for her husband, he felt no loyalty whatsoever to Wanda Higgins and, having formed a shrewd assessment of Madam Bulldog's character, wanted to offer advice about her before they met. Glancing at a drawer, he continued, 'If you would care to look over the accounts and records we have kept—?'

'There's no rush for that, as far as I'm concerned,' the blonde stated airily. 'I'd sooner settle things with

114

Gavin Standish over to the Cattlemen's Bank and put some business to Saul Berstein, Dutchy Schmidt and Thel Whitwell, then talk to that young newspaperman from the *Tennyson Times* like I promised I would last night, before I find out how well you and Joe Turner've been living since Maxie Higgins lit out for Cowtown.'

'I fear, the way we've been cooking the books, you'll *never* be able to find out how we have each laid aside tidy sums against our old age,' Scrope warned, deducing from what would have been a slanderous suggestion if made by a person like Wanda Higgins that the blonde considered him sufficient of a friend to say it without meaning any offense. As he was making a response in kind, he wondered what she might be wanting with the local tailor, builder and owner of the town's largest general store, to whom he had introduced her the previous evening. 'There is one point I feel we should settle before she arrives, however. In addition to the saloon, there is—!'

'It'll have to wait, Counselor,' the blonde interrupted, cocking her head towards the door through which she had entered. 'Unless I'm mistaken, I'd say your other *guest* has shown up.'

Also having heard a feminine voice speaking loudly in the outer office and recognizing it, the attorney nodded agreement.

Without waiting to be announced by Rosemary Scrope, Wanda Higgins threw open the connecting door and made her entrance.

Looking from the blonde to the new arrival, Scrope decided which of them he would have selected as the new owner of the Hide And Horn Saloon if he had been unaware of the situation. The attire worn by the former, while stylish and complimentary to her buxom build, was such she might have been mistaken for the wife of a prominent citizen thereby qualifying for the category of 'good' woman on that account. On the other hand, the red head had on a revealing dress—its bright colours far from tastefully blended—and osten-

115

tatious jewellery more suited to the less than respectable theatrical circles from which she had originated than to the supposedly acceptable female member of the community in a Texas' town of moderate size.

'Good morning, Mrs. Higgins,' the attorney said, but his voice was subtly different to what it had been when he had addressed his other visitor upon her arrival. Indicating her as she rose from the chair she had taken, he went on, 'May I present Madam Bulldog?'

'*Madam Bulldog*?' the red head repeated, running what was clearly a disdainful gaze over the other woman and pointedly ignoring the right hand extended in her direction.

'*Mrs. Higgins*?' the blonde countered blandly. 'Are you Maxie's *wife*?'

'I'm not his *mother*!' Wanda hissed, bristling like an alley cat scenting a rival on its territory.

'I didn't think you were,' Madam claimed, exuding a seeming innocence, and sitting down. 'It's just that I didn't think Maxie had very good *taste* when we met. But now I'm sure he *hasn*—that I was *wrong*.'

'Will you have a seat, Mrs. Higgins?' Scrope suggested, deciding Madam had won the opening exchange. Waiting until his offer was accepted, he continued, 'Now, exactly what can I do for you?'

'You mean you don't *know* why I'm here?' the red head asked sardonically.

'I know nothing whatsoever about *your* business,' the attorney asserted, wanting to establish that he considered only Maxwell and not Wanda Higgins was his client. 'However, I presume it has to do with your husband having lost the Hide And Horn Saloon in the poker game known as "the Big One", at the Silver Bell Saloon at Fort Worth, to my *client*, who reserves her right to be known only by the alias, 'Madam Bulldog''. Am I correct?'

'You know god damned well you are!' the beautiful and statuesque woman replied, without so much as a

116

glance at the buxom blonde, her cheeks reddening under the excessively applied make up. 'Is it *true*?'

'Is what *true*?' Scrope inquired, exuding a sombre lack of comprehension.

'You know what I mean all right, god damn it!' Wanda snapped, her never too stable temper rising.

'If you mean, did the loss take place at the venue and in the fashion I mentioned,' the attorney answered, also giving no indication of knowing there was anybody other than himself and the red head in the office, 'Not having been present when these events took place, I cannot, from personal observation, say whether they did, or did not. However, I have examined all the documents pertaining to the transfer of ownership and am satisfied they are valid.'

'Suppose I say that I aim to have somebody else take a look at them?' Wanda challenged, her manner suggesting she expected to meet with a refusal.

'That is your prerogative, Mrs. Higgins, which neither I nor my client would wish to deny you the right to exercise,' Scrope answered. 'Naturally, however, we would not be prepared to allow you to take them out of my custody.'

'*Naturally*!' the red head sniffed. 'But you'll be willing to let me have, say Counselor Grimsdyke from Garnett, look them over?'

'As I said, that is *your* prerogative and we would not think of denying it,' the attorney confirmed. 'However, I feel I should warn you that, in my opinion, you will merely be wasting your time and money by doing so. All the documents are attested to by men of unimpeachable honesty and integrity, with whom I am personally acquainted to the extent that I know their signatures and seals.'

'That's as *maybe*!' Wanda said, her manner offensive, as the feeling she was being outmanoeuvred grew. 'But Maxie was a damned good poker player and I can't believe *anybody*, especially a *woman*, would get

117

him to lose so heavily he'd have to use the saloon to pay her off.'

'*Can't* believe,' Madam put in, responding to the glance she received from Scrope and interpreting it correctly. 'Or *won't*?'

'My husband was a damned good poker player—!' the red head began.

'He wasn't better than *fair*, at best, and I reckon *you* know that as well as I found out,' the blonde corrected. 'And, which being, he was way out of his class when he decided to sit in on the Big One.'

'And *you* were in a class to sit in on it?'

'I came out winning, which sort of makes it look like I was.'

'There's another *possibility*!'

'Do tell.'

'I've heard about women being used to sucker a feller into a game when it was knowed he wasn't anywhere near good enough to play in it.'

'And you reckon that's what happened to Mr. Higgins?'

'I'm not saying it *was*!' Wanda stated, deciding to resist the temptation to make a direct accusation of complicity. The Big One at the Silver Bell Saloon had a well deserved reputation for the strict honesty with which it was operated. 'Only, when a feller's alone on vacation, he gets to feeling lonely and's fair game for getting suckered into things by a woman!'

'A *married* man doesn't often go off on a vacation *alone*,' Madam countered, seeming to be growing calmer the more heated the red head was showing signs of becoming. 'And, every time I hear a *wife* saying something like *that*, it's most always because she's trying to make folks believe it wasn't *her* fault that he went off *alone* for his vacation. Especially should he get suckered into something by another woman.'

'Why you—!' Wanda spat out, rising suddenly and sending her chair skidding behind her. Then, making a clearly visible effort to keep at least some semblance of control over her temper, she went on viciously, 'If I wasn't a *lady*, I'd ram that god-damned lie down your throat!'

'Well now, it can't be said I've ever even *pretended* to be a lady,' the blonde replied, remaining seated and, although ready to take whatever measures might be required to defend herself if attacked, looking completely unmoved by the rage being directed her way. 'But any time you want to *try* and ram anything down *my* throat, just say the word and we'll go off some place, only the *two of us*, so you can make a stab at doing it!'

For a few seconds, which seemed to be extending for a much greater period to the fascinated and, for once, speechless attorney, Wanda stood quivering with a fury almost too savage to withhold!

Thinking of the preparations she had been making to avenge herself upon the saloongirl who had come to be on most intimate terms with her husband, more because her ego was hurt by the thought that he preferred somebody else than out of any affection for him, the red head was tempted to accept the challenge. Before she could do so, aroused by the remembrance of how Moses Stern had fared when in contention against the blonde, a nagging uncertainty began to assail her. She had discounted his claim that he had been attacked when he was not looking, and she realized that, for him to have been overcome in such a fashion as he had described, implied considerable strength and skill. Therefore, having no desire to chance suffering a defeat, she found herself growing disinclined to take up the gauntlet as she was no longer satisfied the odds would be in her favour.

'Surely you don't expect *me* to come down to *your* level?' Wanda gritted out as she reached her decision. She allowed her clenched hands to sink to her sides.

'It was *your* idea to start ramming what you reckon to be lies down my throat,' Madam replied, having noticed how the other woman had adopted fists

119

instead of crooking fingers ready to grab hair or start scratching as was more generally the feminine tactics under such conditions. 'I was only telling you how I felt about it. What you reckon you should do is up to you.'

'I can see there's no point in me staying here any longer!' the red head informed the attorney, looking at him with an intensity which was clearly meant to exclude the blonde. 'You'll be hearing from Counselor Grimsdyke either Thursday or Friday, depending on how soon I can get hold of him.'

'As you wish!' Scrope assented, not without relief as he had been expecting the meeting to erupt into physical violence between the two women.

'How soon does *she* want to have me thrown out of the house?' Wanda went on, still refraining with an effort from so much as glancing at the person to whom she was referring.

'What house is that?' Madam could not prevent herself from inquiring, despite having decided it might be advisable to allow the lawyer to conclude the interview.

'My *home*!' the red head explained, unable to keep her eyes from the other woman any longer. 'Or didn't my husband tell you he was gambling *that* away along with the saloon?'

'He didn't,' the blonde answered and darted a puzzled look at Scrope. 'All our bet covered was the Hide And Horn Saloon. There wasn't any mention of a house.'

'It is part of his property, though,' the attorney pointed out and hoped the antagonism which he sensed Madam was feeling towards the red head would not prevent her from making an offer that he would have advised, as a means of avoiding criticism when the news was spread, if he had been given the opportunity earlier.

'Not as far as I'm concerned,' the blonde declared, deciding just as the lawyer had hoped she would, even without needing his prompting. 'All I won was the saloon. No house came into the bet and I don't want any part of it.'

'And I'll be "somethinged" before I'll accept *charity* from the likes of *you*!' Wanda claimed, once again realizing she was being out-manoeuvred. By announcing she was to be deprived of her home as well as the lucrative business, with which her husband had been compelled to part after being cajoled into a game of poker against players of far greater skill, she had hoped to enlist the sympathy of at least some of the local community. Trying to salvage something from the scheme, she went on in tones of bitterness, 'So I'll be out of my *home* as quickly as possible.'

'Whether you go, or stay, is entirely up to you and none of my never-mind,' Madam asserted, guessing the motivation behind the insistence to quit the premises. 'Counsellor Scrope here will let you have the deeds for it and then you can do what you like.'

'Shall I have my daughter drop them around when they're prepared, Mrs. Higgins?' the attorney inquired, showing none of the delight he was feeling over the way in which the blonde had treated the issue. 'I can have them ready and delivered by sundown.'

'You'll have to send them to Counselor Grimsdyke in Garnett,' the red head instructed, making the pronouncement as if every word was leaving a very bad taste in her mouth. 'Because, seeing's how I wouldn't live in any "mother-something" house *she* reckons she has the right to *give* me, I'll be moving there this afternoon.'

'Very well,' Scrope assented. 'However, should you ever ask to come and see me in the future, I'd be greatly obliged if you would clean up your language.'

'Why?' Wanda hissed. 'Are you scared it might offend *her*?'

'*Girlie*,' Madam said, before the attorney could reply. 'I've heard more bad language and, in the right time

121

and place, can put tongue to more profanity than you've heard even in the kind of places you've come from. There's only one thing stopping me proving it right now. This *isn't* the time and place, with a young woman able to hear it next door.'

'Go to hell, both of you!' the red head spat out and turned to leave with less assumed majesty than she had arrived.

'I'd say that's what I've heard called "leaving in high dudgeon",' the blonde commented, after the main entrance to the attorney's place of business was closed with a bang. 'Danged if I haven't always wanted to see it done.'

'She's not the nicest woman I've ever come across,' Scrope remarked. 'And there'll be more than me delighted to see the back of her around town.'

'You reckon she'll leave then?' Madam asked.

'She'll go all right,' the attorney assessed. 'From what I know of her, she'd die rather than stay here with folks knowing that it's only because you didn't take the house as well as the saloon. For all that, I'd go very carefully. Unless I'm mistaken, you haven't seen the last of her. Or, at least, she won't give up trying to get back the saloon as easily as it seems she is doing.'

'You mean she reckons that lawyer of hers down to Garnett might be able to do something about it?' the blonde suggested.

'All he can tell her is what I've already said; the whole affair was done legally and above board,' Scrope replied. 'But I can't see her being willing to accept its gone because of that.'

'You mean she might decide to come and try to *take* it back?' Madam asked.

'Not personally,' the attorney answered. 'But you can bet she'll be willing to try some other way of doing it.'

CHAPTER ELEVEN

All Sociable And Friendly

'Take *that!*' Wanda Higgins ejaculated savagely, thinking of Madam Bulldog while doing so. Then she went on, in similar snorting gasps, 'And *that!* And *that!*'

Before starting to speak, the beautiful and curvaceous red head had been moving lightly on the balls of her bare feet with something like dancing steps, except they were not for such an innocuous purpose. The first two words were in accompaniment to her left hand, closed into a fist, being driven forward. Encased in a special type of black leather glove, it impacted firmly against the bosom region of a large sack—packed solidly with straw and forming the shape of a well endowed feminine figure—which was suspended from the ceiling of a bedroom converted into a simply equipped gymnasium.

Delivered skilfully and with evidence of its not inconsiderable power, the blow was followed by an equally well executed right hook up into the *solar plexus* region of her now moving target and a left cross swing to the side of the 'head'. They were sent in rapid succession, each being punctuated by an identical exclamation. Nor did this bring the efforts of the woman to an end. Bobbing, ducking, weaving her upper body and making occasional blocking motions with alternate arms, she continued to attack the specially made punching bag she was circling with an energy and vigour which would have surprised most of those who had become acquainted with her generally slothful nature.

The uncharacteristic behaviour of the red head had come about, on this occasion, as a result of her most unsatisfactory interview with the new owner of the Hide And Horn Saloon and Aloysius P. Scrope!

Having swept out of the attorney's offices in an even worse temper than she had risen with that morning, Wanda had hurried back to the house, by the most direct route, so as to avoid meeting anybody who might wish to talk about the situation in which she found herself. Suffering from no illusions with regards to her popularity where the majority of the population were concerned, she had felt sure any commiserations would be far from sincere. Finding the young reporter for the *Tennyson Times* waiting on the front porch, she had refused to comment about the loss of the saloon and her plans for the future. However, as she had realized there might soon be a need for sympathetic comments on its pages, she had refrained from dismissing him with the torrent of profanity which had come close to bursting around his head, and had promised she would supply all the requisite information when less busy.

Going into the sitting-room, the red head had been only slightly more communicative with Leo Wallace and Moses Stern. They had had to be content with being told that the meeting with the blonde and Scrope—both of whom were described in profanely insulting terms—had produced nothing beyond what they had anticipated. Then, without offering any reason, she had told her hulking brother to fetch Barry Norman and Herbert Lang, but to ensure they were not seen entering the house. Asked how quickly she wanted them to come, she had replied there was no hurry as she intended to go and 'work out' in the bedroom. Knowing what was implied by this, the deposed head bouncer had set off without further questions, and the gambler had also considered it inadvisable to attempt to satisfy his curiosity.

Being all too aware of the lecherous nature of her half-brother, having been subjected to less than filial attentions from him in the past, Wanda had locked the door and left the key in its hole before starting to disrobe for her 'work out'. She would not have been in the least embarassed by the thought of him watching her through the aperture, despite being reduced to a state of near nudity, but she took a perverse delight in preventing him from having the pleasure of doing so. Then, wearing only brief—for that day and age— bright red satin drawers trimmed by frilly black lace, she had donned a pair of four ounce padded gloves such as were used in the kind of scientific boxing which was fast replacing the old style of crude and, at best, semi-skilful bare knuckle pugilism.

Shortly after starting to carry out her unconventional activity, the red head had discovered that the exercise helped her to shake off a state of anger more economically than—as had frequently been her habit in the past—smashing furniture and crockery. Furthermore, she had found it helped her to think more clearly about whatever problem was causing the bad temper. With these motives in mind, she had set about relieving the stress of her pent up emotions by battering at the punching bag which had been specially made to meet her requirements.

Regardless of trying to decide what might be done to regain control of the lucrative lost business, Wanda was forcing herself to remember the lessons received from a professional boxing trainer found for her by County Sheriff Lloyd Bowman—one of the very few people let into her secret—on hearing of her intention to take revenge upon Viola Grant. There was, however, one major difference to her efforts. While concentrating upon the coordination of footwork, defensive tactics and throwing punches with accuracy, all her strength and precision, her hatred was now diverted to the buxom blonde who had humiliated and made her back down in front of the attorney.

After about two minutes of the strenuous activity, a knock on the door caused the freely perspiring red head to lower her hands and move away from the punching bag. Breathing heavily, she pulled off the gloves by inserting each in turn between her thighs. With this done, she collected and donned a more substantial robe than that worn in the morning. Then she opened the door and glowered at the two men standing outside.

'Well?' Wanda asked, drawing malicious satisfaction from the disappointment on Wallace's face when he saw that she had concealed herself from neck level before appearing.

'The fellers're downstairs, Wan'!' Stern announced, as if collecting and delivering the pair of hard-cases was a feat requiring considerable skill.

'Say I'll be down to see them in a few minutes,' the woman commanded. 'Then go and tell Josh Gilmore I want to see him and, after you've done that, fetch the horses from the livery barn and hitch up my surrey.'

'Are you figuring to go and meet Lloyd Bowman on the trail, Wan'?' Wallace inquired, remembering his half-sister had mentioned arranging for the sheriff to follow in case his assistance might be required to regain possession of the saloon.

'We'll meet him along the way,' the red head answered. 'But he'll be coming here alone. We're going to be staying down to Garnett for at least a few days.'

'What're we going there for?' Stern asked.

'*We're* not going, just Leo and me,' Wanda corrected, but with no trace of apology. 'You're staying in Tennyson.'

'Doing what?' the hulking man demanded.

'Working for Gilmore,' the red head explained. 'Or so everybody'll think. What you'll really be doing is keeping an eye on things around here and letting us know what's doing.'

'Aw hell!' Stern protested. 'I don't need to go to work for Gilmore to do *that*!'

'How the "something" do you expect to do it? By hanging around the front door of the Hide or listening outside the office?' Wanda demanded, her manner viciously sarcastic. 'You have to have a reason for staying on, seeing Leo and I'll have spread the word we've gone and don't aim to come back.'

'Yeah—But—!' the hulking man began.

'Don't worry!' the red head interrupted, all too aware of her brother's disinclination to expend physical effort. 'You won't be expected to do too much *work*, if he'll go along with what I've got in mind.'

'Why don't you get Rudy Schanz to take me on?' Stern suggested, feeling sure the blacksmith would expect more than a token appearance of work, regardless of what might be promised to the contrary.

'It'll cost *me* enough talking Gilmore into having you,' the red head replied, suspecting the only way she could persuade the blacksmith to agree was by offering to supplement her brother's wages. 'Schanz would want me to hand over *all* your god-damned pay and, him being married, I can't get around him the same way I can Gilmore. Now get the hell out of here and do as I told you.'

'Sure, Wan'!' Stern assented sullenly and turned to shamble away, muttering inaudibly.

'What've you got on that tricky mind of your'n, Wan'?' Wallace asked, being aware that the bouts of violent exercise acted as a stimulant to thought for his half-sister.

'Do you think those two useless bastards downstairs would *kill* somebody?'

'They've done it before.'

'Would they gun down a woman?'

'I shouldn't reckon, knowing them, they'd give a shit whether it was a man or a woman, so long as they

127

reckoned they could get away with it,' Wallace assessed, and gave a nod as he realized what had been implied by the question. 'You mean *her* at the Hide?'

'I mean *her* at the Hide,' Wanda confirmed. 'Would they be willing to gun her down, knowing it'll be Lloyd Bowman and not Collier who'll be looking into why they did it?'

'Hell, yes!' the gambler declared. 'After what she done to them last night and with that going for them, they'd be ready to take her down.'

'Then go give them a couple of drinks and keep them remembering what she did to them while I get dressed,' the red head instructed. 'It's time they did something to earn the pay I've—!'

'Hey, Wan'!' Stern called from downstairs. 'Them two old bastards from the Hide've come asking about the old faro table.'

'Tell them Leo took it with him when he lit out this morning,' the beautiful woman replied. 'Say I'll have him send it back when we get his table passed down to us in Garnett, but not before.'

'Sure, Wan'!' the hulking man replied, having no idea why he was to supply such false information—the original table being in the storm cellar—but considering it advisable to do as he was ordered.

'What's the idea, Wan'?' Wallace inquired.

'Whether those two take her out or not,' the red head answered. 'It'll make Lloyd's work easier happen he can say she'd got crooked gambling gear on the premises.'

* * *

'Everything's going smooth as the skin on a baby's butt, boss!' Joseph Turner reported, running an appreciative gaze over the new owner of the Hide And Horn saloon as he met her at the door of the wide staircase she had just descended. ' 'Cept that everybody's stopped to look at *you*. Which I can't say's I blame them for doing.'

'Go on!' Madam Bulldog replied, smiling and not unflattered by the response from her floor manager. 'You're only saying that 'cause it's *true!*'

There was more than an attempt at 'apple polishing' behind the greeting given by Turner!

It was, in fact, a point of view shared by every man in the bar-room!

No longer was the blonde clad in the demure attire in which she had presented herself to the citizens ever since her arrival at Tennyson!

Bare headed, except for the spray of white ibis feathers attached to her neatly piled blonde hair, Madam had on a gown made from shiny black satin which clung to her buxomly curvaceous figure like a second skin. Apart from what a later generation would call a 'halter neck' of no great width, it left bare her shoulders, arms and back to waist level. Its décolleté was lower and more daring than any worn by Wanda Higgins, even when setting out to offend the susceptibilities of the Ladies Guild For Civic Betterment. Slit up the right side almost to the hip, its skirt displayed her sturdy legs. They were encased in black silk stockings supported by frilly red garters and offered just a glimpse of the white skin between the stocking tops and whatever nether garments she wore, which were obviously not extensive. Silver high heeled shoes were on her feet. Although wearing more jewellery than she had up to now, it was neither excessive nor ostentatious and there were no rings of any kind on her no longer gloved hands. Seeming somewhat incongruous with such elegant attire, a black leather gunbelt of excellent design and with the ivory handled Webley Bulldog revolver in its cross draw holster at the left encircled her trim waist.

Nothing about the attractive and attention drawing appearance presented by the blonde gave a hint of how busy she had been all afternoon!

Returning to the saloon after the meeting with Wanda Higgins and her attorney, Madam had collected the brown pigskin valise from the safe in her private office. Taking it to the Cattlemen's Bank, she had deposited the large sun of money it contained and had made arrangements for an even greater amount to be transferred from a similar establishment in Fort Worth. Having told the owner, Gavin Standish, of certain plans she had for improving her business and securing his support for part of them, she had had lunch with the reporter for the *Tennyson Times*. Annoyed by his treatment at the hands of the red head, the offer of information later notwithstanding, he had decided to give the blonde the better of the coverage he would be presenting to his editor. Her conferences with Saul Bernstein, Otto 'Dutchy' Schmidt and Thel Whitwell had proved equally productive and, hearing what was wanted from them, they had gone away further convinced her presence in the town would be beneficial to them.

The tailor had started work, measuring those of the gambling staff who could not find a better than passable fit amongst the black shirts and trousers Madam had brought with her. Showing an equal enthusiasm, the builder had taken dimensions for equipping a room in which the gamblers would change before commencing operations, with facilities for them to leave their valuables locked in individual boxes. He had also satisfied himself that he would be able to fit the douche bath she had requested, although doing so would entail adding another room to her living accommodation on the second floor. Not only had the storekeeper been able to supply her immediate needs, but he had also been promised that much of the saloon's future requirements would be purchased through him instead of—as had been the case with the previous owner—obtained direct from distributors or via a rival establishment in the county seat.

With the arrangements for future improvements

completed, Madam had set about making preparations for the business of the evening. Her hope that she would be able to exchange the faro tables had come to nothing. She felt sure that a lie had been told as the reason for Leo Wallace being unable to change them, but she had not taken the matter further. There were sufficient clean decks of cards, aided by the entire stock from Whitwell's store, and honest dice available for all the games to be run as she required. Furthermore, a supply having arrived two days earlier—although not being displayed on the shelves—there was enough beer and liquor of various kinds to satisfy the needs of any normal flow of customers.

The last tasks carried out by the blonde before changing into her present attire had had to do with a project which she hoped to bring to fruition in the not too distant future. Reading the message and the names to which it was addressed, the telegraph operator at the Wells Fargo depot could not hide his curiosity and interest. Admitting she had high hopes that all the well known personalities with whom she was communicating would accept her invitation, she had no doubt that—rules to the contrary notwithstanding—he would inform his cronies and they, in turn, would spread the news around the town. With that contingency in mind, she had sought out and informed Town Marshal Tune Collier of her intentions and explained the strict rules she meant to enforce to ensure the good behaviour of everybody concerned. Admitting these should have the desired effect, he had wished her well with the enterprise.

'The house men are looking elegant,' Madam remarked, glancing around at the various gambling games. 'How're they settling in?'

'Well enough,' Turner replied. 'Anyways, I don't reckon any of them're likely to try anything for the first couple of nights or so at least.'

'Likely not,' the blonde admitted, but her manner suggested caution.

'Anyways, unless they fetch along their own,' the floor manager went on, 'There isn't a marked deck, crooked dice or usuable slick cup in the house for them to try flim-flamming the customers.'

'Howdy there, Madam Bulldog, if you aren't a sight for sore eyes—or any other kind,' Joshua Gilmore greeted, coming over before she could say her thoughts were not upon the *customers* being 'flim-flammed' by the house men. Extending his right hand and running a lascivious gaze over her, he went on, 'I hear tell's how you're fixing to run a game here like the Big One at the Silver Bell in Cowtown.'

'I've asked some of the crowd I've played against there to drop by and give it a whirl on my ground,' the blonde admitted, accepting the offered hand for a briefer shake than was intended by the blacksmith.

'Poker Alice, Madame Moustache, Pappy Ben Maverick, among others,' Gilmore listed. 'Now that's the kind of company I'd admire to sit in with!'

'It's open to anybody who's willing to go along with the house rules,' Madam claimed, deciding never to send any confidential messages in the care of the Wells Fargo telegraphist unless she had made him sure of the penalty for such indiscretion.

'*House rules?*' the blacksmith repeated, glancing at the group of his cronies who were hovering within hearing distance and to whom he had boasted that he would win over the blonde as he had many another woman, married or single.

'You have to let me know how much loss you can stand, show *proof* that you're good for it and put two thousand dollars in the Cattlemen's Bank as surety against your good behaviour, not only in the game, but *everywhere* in town.'

'Hell, I live *here*. That last won't apply to *me!*'

'It applies to *everybody*, no matter who they are or where they live,' Madam declared and decided she could exaggerate a trifle under the circumstances. 'Gavin Standish and Tune Collier are only *two* I've told about it who float their stick along with me on doing it that way.'

'Is that how they run the Big One?' Gilmore inquired sullenly, forgetting that he had frequently told his cronies of his regular participation in the famous poker game.

'Just about,' the blonde confirmed. 'But the idea of having the surety against good behaviour is all *mine*.'

'That being, it's all right with me,' the blacksmith asserted and put on what he fondly imagined to be a friendly and charm filled smile. 'Only how's about you and me talking some more about it over *drinks* and dinner?'

'*Drinks*?'

'There ain't nothing I know's better for getting folks all friendly and sociable.'

'By golly, you're *right* at that!' Madam declared, much to the surprise of Turner who had expected a refusal. She noticed the nudges and glances passing amongst Gilmore's cronies and nodded towards the wide staircase to the second floor. 'We could go up to my rooms for it, unless you'd sooner use somewhere else.'

'Your rooms will do fine!' the blacksmith accepted, delighted by the apparent ease with which, it seemed, he would be able to make good the claim to his cronies that he would seduce the blonde as well as Wanda Higgins on the same day; the latter having succumbed as part of the deal to give the impression of his having hired Moses Stern.

Allowing Gilmore to take her by the arm, Madam told a waiter to accompany them to the sitting-room of her accommodation. Once there, she ordered food and the best whiskey in the house to be fetched for them. With these delivered and the waiter dismissed, nothing was seen or heard of them for over two hours. Then the door through which they had disappeared was opened. Looking upwards from the table they were occupying, Gilmore's cronies received a surprise.

They had been discussing what they believed he would be doing after having plied her with alcohol until she could not resist. However, showing no sign of intoxication or the dishevelment which would have accrued from being subjected to the behaviour they had anticipated, it was she and not the blacksmith who emerged.

'Hey, fellers,' the blonde said, having returned to the bar-room and crossed to the table where the 'sports' were sitting practically open mouthed in their amazement. 'You'd best go tote your *amigo* home to bed, he can't take his liquor nearly as well as he thinks.'

CHAPTER TWELVE

"Eleven Dollar Bill"

'What do you reckon about Matt MacDonald?' Madam Bulldog inquired, nodding towards the busy *vingt-un* table.

'I don't reckon he's forgot or forgive' you for knocking him down that first night,' Joseph Turner replied, looking in the same direction. 'But he's not said, nor done, anything I could complain about and, seeing as how those fancy duds you've got the gamblers wearing don't let him sneak any of the cash into his pockets for his-self, I can't see him ringing in a deck of readers when all he'll be doing is making money for the house.'

It was Saturday and the fourth evening of the Hide And Horn Saloon being owned by the blonde. Despite the questions she had put to the floor manager, all in all, she had no complaints over the way things had gone. Not only had she been informed by Turner that business was showing an improvement over that done under the proprietorship of Maxwell Higgins, but most of the people to whom she had sent messages had replied, accepting her invitation to participate in a poker game for high stakes and under similar rules to those of the Big One at the Silver Bell Saloon in Fort Worth.

As she had promised Town Marshal Tune Collier, during the first interview in the offices of Aloysius P.

Scrope, Madam had run her property in an exemplary fashion. Although still compelled to use the specially adapted faro table, having failed to contact Leo Wallace—who she knew had left for Garnett with Wanda Higgins, albeit later than was implied when she had sent her swampers to the house to arrange for the exchange—she had ensured all gambling on the premises was operated with complete honesty. She had also insisted upon high standards of conduct from her employees, male and female, whether in or outside the saloon.

Possessing a knack for treating them all in an equally friendly fashion, which nevertheless did not extend to permitting liberties to be taken at her expense, the blonde had gained respect and admiration from the majority of her customers. Her attitude tended to keep trouble to a minimum and, so far, only one thing had threatened to disrupt the pleasant atmosphere she had created.

Arriving during the next evening after his failure to get drunk and seduce Madam Bulldog, Joshua Gilmore had been informed there would be no further acceptance of invitations to have 'drinks and dinner'. Nor, in view of how the first attempt had turned out, was he inclined to try and bring about a change of mind. Instead, he had sought revenge by joining a game of poker in which she was playing. Finding her vastly more competent than the man from whom he had won the blacksmith's shop, he might have been grateful that table stakes were in force.[1] As it was, he had lost all the inconsiderable sum he was carrying and left the table in a bitter mood. However, possessing a broad streak of caution, he had been too wise to make his

1. 'Table stakes'. A rule by which a participant in a game of poker is restricted to staking whatever money is carried on the person. This precludes sending out for added funds and attempting to borrow from other players, or the onlookers, a common cause of dissent when the rule is not enforced. J.T.E.

resentment known by physical aggression. Leaving the bar-room, he had not been back again. Nor, out of sympathy for him—or more likely not wishing to arouse his animosity,—had any of his cronies continued to give custom to the Hide And Horn Saloon.

In addition to improving what a later generation would call her 'image' where the saloon was concerned, the blonde had wasted no time in setting about gaining acceptance by the community in general. Although she had not mentioned the matter, Scrope had made the true facts generally known and had discredited a rumour that she had forced Wanda Higgins to quit her house. He had also established that, although he had pointed out she was not legally bound to do so, she had insisted upon settling bills which Maxwell Higgins had left owing to various local business men. Without having been approached, she had made donations to both of the town's churches. She had said that she would not attend either, but would keep her premises closed on Sundays and religious holidays. From what she had been told by her attorney, she had made a favourable impression on the incumbent of each place of worship.

Even if there had not been sufficient time for Madam to have gained the unqualified approbation of the Ladies Guild For Civic Betterment, she had skilfully avoided antagonizing them. While none would have expressed approval openly, they admitted amongst themselves that—no matter how she dressed inside the saloon—she took care never to offend their susceptibilities in public. Unlike Wanda Higgins, whose atire and manners had frequently bordered upon the risque, despite ostensibly being a 'good' woman, the blonde was always clad and behaved in a decorous fashion when off her premises, insisting her female employees took an equal care to do so.

Despite the gambling staff apparently having accepted the strictures she had imposed, the blonde had been wary. However, of them all, only Matthew

McDonald had struck her as being worthy of deserving her attention. There was nothing she could put her finger on, but an instinct she had learned to trust warned her that he was the most likely to make trouble in some way. Nor, regardless of his having carried out his duties at the *vingt-un* table adequately, could she dispel the feeling.

'You're right about that,' Madam admitted, then nodded to where Scrope, the banker and three other businessmen were entering. 'Anyways, here come my pigeons. I reckon we'll use that table over there, Joe.'

'Sure thing, boss,' Turner assented, noticing in which direction his employer was pointing. 'Will you be needing me?'

'Only happen one of those good old boys catches me dealing seconds,' the blonde answered with a smile.

For all her apparent acceptance that all was well there, the floor manager saw Madam was selecting the chair nearest to and offering a good view of the *vingt-un* table. What was more, as she commenced a low stake—yet skilfully played—game of poker with the newcomers, she devoted some of her attention to it without making the scrutiny obvious. There were five players, four cowhands and a lean and poorly dressed town dweller. However, regardless of his attire which suggested he was far from affluent, the latter had a fair amount of money in front of him.

While playing poker, the blonde continued to keep the town dweller under observation. She noticed that every time he made a bet, he always used several bills, the denominations of which she could not see. Furthermore, despite the cowhands each announcing the amount being wagered, he did not make a similar declaration. Nor, although supposed to insist upon it, did McDonald ask him to do so. What was more, every time he lost a hand, he would ask for a ten dollar bill to be changed in spite of there being money before him.

'Excuse me, boys!' Madam requested, after about an

138

hour had elapsed, unable to restrain her curiosity any longer. 'I'm just going to circulate a mite.'

'Sure,' assented the attorney, wondering what had been diverting the attention of his client. 'It'll give one of us poor suckers a chance to win a pot or two.'

'I once heard the biggest thrill of gambling is losing,' the blonde claimed. 'So, not being one for thrills, I always like to let my friends have them instead of me.'

'With friends like you,' Gavin Standish put in, calculating he had lost five dollars and twenty-five cents since sitting down. 'I'll soon be too poor to *afford* enemies.'

'Whoever heard of a banker having *friends*?' the blonde countered and strolled away in an apparently nonchalant fashion.

Making a circuit of the bar-room, as she had made a habit of doing regularly, Madam still kept a surreptitious watch on the *vingt-un* table while exchanging comments with various customers. Followed by many eyes, as she was wearing a scarlet gown in the same fashion as the black dress she had worn on the second night, she timed her arrival to coincide with the town dweller losing a hand.

'You're doing real well, Matt,' the blonde declared, after the middle sized and overweight gambler had drawn in the stakes. 'Hell, I've just remembered I need some cash to pay a marker to the Counselor. So I'll take what I need from here.'

Before McDonald could speak, Madam picked up a pile of bills which included those taken from the town dweller. Giving no indication that she had noticed the consternation both of them started to display, she walked away from the table. Catching the attention of Turner in passing, she signalled for him to join her. They met at the door of her private office and, without offering any explanation, she led the way inside. Wondering why he had been summoned, he watched her place the money on her desk and start to examine each bill in turn.

139

'What's up, boss?' the floor manager inquired, as the blonde stiffened and gave a low exclamation.

'So *that's* what they were up to!' Madam breathed. 'By golly, it's a new one on me!'

'How do you mean?' Turner wanted to know.

At first sight, the bill extended towards the floor manager by his employer appeared to be valued at one dollar. However, on her turning it over, its denomination was that of a ten.[2]

'It's the neatest god-damned caper I've come across in many a year!' Madam stated, with something closer to admiration than anger in her voice.

'This's been done *real* carefully, I'll admit,' Turner replied, his tone puzzled, examining the bill and discovering it to be genuine ten and one dollar bills stuck exactly back to back. 'Only I still don't see how it's used.'

'It goes this way, I reckon,' the blonde began, 'The townie—!'

'He's called "Shardlow", or some such, but it's likely a summer name. Hangs around on the fringes of Gilmore's bunch.'

' "Shardlow", then, puts down nine singles and this "eleven dollar bill", let's call it for the same of argument, is amongst them with the buck side upwards making ten. If he wins, good ole Matt scoops in the pile, turns it over and——!'

'Pays out the bet as if it was for nineteen bucks!' Turner finished, some understand-of the situation coming at last. Then he let out a furious growl and went on, 'Hell's fire, boss, that means Shardlow gets it at even money, or two to one if he's holding a natural!'[3]

---

2. *For the benefite of readers unfamiliar with that country, all bills of lower denominations of United States' currency are the same size and colour. J.T.E.*

3. *'Natural'; used in this context, a score of twenty-one made by adding the value of only two cards, with kings, queens and jacks counting ten and aces eleven. Even at the period of this narrative,*

140

'That's the way it goes,' Madam confirmed.

'But what happens when he loses?' the floor manager asked and waved the 'eleven dollar bill'. 'How many of these do they have?'

'Only the one,' the blonde explained. 'Matt scoops up the money, making sure he keeps an eye on and extracts the "eleven". Then he hands it back when Shardlow gets a ten spot changed. That way, they're only out nine bucks in ten for a loser and haul down either nineteen or thirty-eight every time he pulls a win.'

'Son-of-a-bitch!' Turner ejaculated. 'How long've they been at it, boss?'

'Only tonight, I reckon,' Madam estimated and described the events which had drawn her attention to what was happening, concluding, 'I've been watching Matt and haven't seen Shardlow at his table until tonight.'

'Looks like we're going to have to pick up his toes, boss,' the floor manager commented, not without a slight trace of satisfaction in his demeanour, as he had never entirely forgiven the over-weight gambler for having cast unwarranted aspersions upon his relationship with the blonde.

'Just firing him will do,' Madam corrected, being aware of what was implied by the expression used by the burly man, and her manner indicated she would listen to no other suggestions. 'Have him come here so I can do it.'

---

the game of vingt-un—*frequently corrupted to 'vanjohn' by Americans and known as 'pontoon' in the British Commonwealth—was becoming referred to as 'black jack', or the translation from French, 'twenty-one' in the United States. More detailed information regarding the playing of the game is recorded in:* THE WHIP AND THE WAR LANCE. *Incidentally, Sergeant Seamus Patrick 'Paddy' Magoon, q.v., makes a 'guest' appearance in the above mentioned volume. J.T.E.*

'Maybe he won't want to come,' Turner hinted, almost hopefully it seemed to his employer.

'Could be he won't,' the blonde admitted, being just as aware that to be caught out while employing such a trick would almost certainly provoke painful—perhaps even lethal—repercussions in many saloons. 'But we don't want anything that could start the other gamblers to feuding again with the rest of the crew. So tell him, if he comes peaceable, all I aim to do is pay him off and he can go some other place to use his "eleven dollar bill".'

'Whatever you say, boss,' Turner assented, being willing to concede his employer was making her usual good sense. 'Are you going to give it back to him?'

'Hell *no*!' Madam replied with a smile, taking back the 'eleven dollar bill'. 'Let him make another one wherever he figures on trying it next.'

'Aw *shit*!' the floor manager ejaculated, having crossed and opened the door giving access to the barroom and seeing another of the gamblers was now acting as dealer at the *vingt-un* table. 'He hasn't wasted any time!'

'How do you mean?' the blonde inquired, although she could guess.

'Charlie Henderson's handling his table,' Turner informed. 'He must've put in a call for a relief as soon as we came in here. Can't see Shardlow anywhere, either.'

'Lit a shuck, huh?' Madam said, showing neither surprise nor annoyance. Opening a drawer to put in all the money, except the 'eleven dollar bill' which she tucked into a secret pocket on the inside at the right of her gunbelt, she went on, 'Well, that saves needing to pay him off. Come on, my pigeons will be wondering whether I'm figuring on quitting while I'm so far ahead.'

'How much're you taking 'em for, boss?' the floor manager inquired with a grin, knowing the game was for far from high stakes despite being contested most seriously.

'Must be all of nine dollars and fifteen cents,' the blonde estimated. 'Hell, Joe, should I keep on winning that way, I'll be able to retire and travel the world.'

'Aren't you 'shamed to take so much from them poor gentlemen?'

'No more than they was last night when they took me for a whole twelve dollars and forty cents between them.'

'That *much*, huh?' Turner asked.

'Why'd you think I had them back tonight?' Madam queried, as soberly as if discussing a matter of tremendous importance. 'I'm after revenge. Let's go, Joe. Maybe you'd best go and make sure McDonald doesn't take anything except his own gear from the changing room.'

'I'll tend to it, boss,' the floor manager promised. 'Only don't you go losing this place the same way you got it from Maxie.'

'I'll try not to,' the blonde promised.

Leaving the office, Madam and Turner separated. However, as she was making her way across the barroom towards the table at which the poker game was being held, she noticed two men coming through the front entrance. Although she had not seen them since they had left with Leo Wallace on the first night of her occupancy, one being carried by the other, she recognized them as his far from effective bodyguards. They were dressed in much the same fashion and, if their somewhat unsteady gait was any indication, had been drinking more than was seemly. Furthermore, nothing about them suggested their state of intoxication had induced a feeling of good spirits towards the world.

Unless the blonde was doing them an injustice, she considered the newcomers were 'on the prod' and looking for trouble!

What was more, watching the pair coming in her

143

direction, Madam concluded that she was the objective for their less than friendly intentions!

'Can I do something for you, gents?' the blonde asked, as the two men came to a halt a short distance from her. She failed to notice that the red haired saloon girl, Sally, was passing them.

'You're the lousy tail-peddling calico cat's got us fired by Leo Wallace!' Barry Norman announced in a loud voice. 'He wouldn't give us no pay, so we've come to take it from *you*!'

'And don't nobody else make a move!' ordered Herbert Lang, reaching with his left hand to catch Sally by the arm as she was passing. Bringing out and cocking his revolver with the right, he thrust its muzzle against her side and went on. ' 'Cause, if any son-of-a-bitch does, she's going to be dead!'

CHAPTER THIRTEEN

You Being A *Woman* Won't Stop Me

'Do just what he says, all of you!' Madam Bulldog ordered, her voice carrying around the bar-room of the Hide And Horn Saloon in the silence which had suddenly descended. 'This is between me and them!'

Although there were many men present who would have been willing to intercede upon her behalf, including a number of the customers, the instructions given by the buxom blonde were delivered in a tone which warned she expected to be obeyed. This was an even greater inducement to compliance than the threat to the red haired saloon-girl. However, such was the esteem in which the new owner was now held, the general concensus of opinion was that a most painful retribution would be exacted against the two hard-cases if any harm should befall the girl at their hands.

'Now,' Madam went on, looking from Herbert Lang to Barry Norman. 'What's all this *foolishness* about?'

'I told you jusht now!' the unemcumbered man replied loudly, swaying a trifle on his feet and slurring the words, more than he had when first addressing her. 'You got Herb 'n' me fired by Leo Wall-ash and he told ush he wouldn't give ush no pay. So we've come to get it offen you!'

'And what if I won't give it to you?' the blonde inquired, taking two steps and coming to a halt without any objections from either hard-case.

'Then Herb 'n' me's going to take it out of your-sh hide!'

'Why not just *you*, or do you reckon you'll *need* Herb to back your play?'

'Just-sh *me*, you "mother-something" tail peddler!' Norman declared. 'And you being a *woman* won't stop me doing it!'

'I reckon you'd be a heap more likely to back off from me was I a *man*,' Madam claimed, standing apparently relaxed and at ease, with none of the truculence being displayed by the taller hard-case. 'Only you didn't show any too *well* last time you tried to take me.'

Despite her seemingly relaxed and disdainful attitude, the blonde was far from unaware of the danger. What was more, she fully appreciated the ramifications of the situation. For one thing, having had considerable experience with men in various stages of intoxication over the years, she did not believe either hard-case had imbibed enough to be rendered ineffective. In fact, taking into account how they had addressed her on arrival, she felt sure they were completely sober and cognizant with what they were doing.

Remembering an axiom of gun fighters and wanting to test her theory, Madam had made the experiment of stepping closer to Norman.[1] Although a drunken man tended to halt at the distance from which his eyes focussed most clearly, he had not protested. Nor had his slurred speech been consistent and he only inserted words ike 'ush' and 'jusht' as though they were something of an after-thought.

'Watch the fat old bitch, Norm!' Lang advised, also raising his voice so it would carry to everybody present

1. *This axiom was quoted at length by Captain Dustine Edward Marsden 'Dusty' Fog, q.v., to Marvin Eldridge 'Doc' Leroy and Jason 'Rusty' Willis while instructing them in their duties on the first occasion they served as peace officers: see,* QUIET TOWN. *J.T.E.*

146

and be remembered when questions were being asked by the peace officer they had been promised would handle the investigation of the incident. Retaining his hold on Sally's arm and keeping the revolver pressed against her side, he went on, 'That's a man's gun rig she's got on and she reckons to be a regular snake with that fancy white handled hog-leg she's toting.'

'I'll keep that in mind, Herb!' the taller hard-case promised. 'Only it ain't going to stop her handing over what we've got coming to us!'

'I owe you *nothing* and you *know* I don't,' Madam stated. 'But I'll be willing to let you get the hell out of here and not bring Marshal Collier on your damned fool heads, providing you go straight away!'

Feeling sure neither man expected her to pay them the money they claimed had been refused by Wallace, the blonde knew there was nothing to be gained by behaving in a conciliatory fashion. Her main intention was to prevent harm coming to the red haired saloon girl, or anybody else in the bar-room other than herself and the hard-cases. Doubting whether she would gain anything by referring to the local peace officer, especially if she was correct in her assumption over why the pair had come, she had done so only to offer them a way of leaving without attempting to carry out their purpose.

The hope did not materialize!

'You talk big for a fat old lobby lizzy!' Norman sneered. 'Now let's see you back it all the way!'

Confident that he had nothing to fear, disbelieving what he had been told about the speed with which his intended victim had acted on the previous occasion, the hard-case sent his right hand towards the low tied Colt Army Model of 1860 revolver at the conclusion of the words.

Alert for such an action, Madam responded to it at the instant it was commenced!

While reaching across, the blonde was grateful that she had taken sufficient practice to make the movement without needing to think consciously that she was carrying the Webley Bulldog at her waist and not in the shoulder holster worn when outside the saloon.[2] Without even the momentary hesitation such a need to remember would have created, she brought the weapon out of leather.

Regardless of the rapidity with which Madam was moving, she did not allow herself to be flustered. Knowing that manually operating the double action of the Webley gave a fraction of a second advantage, she did just that! However, she neither started to draw back the hammer with her thumb, nor let her right forefinger enter the triggerguard until the muzzle was turning towards Norman. This, those among the onlookers conversant with matters *pistolero* were aware, was a sign that she was very well versed in handling a handgun in the heat of conflict.[3]

Just as his Colt was rising above the lip of its holster, Norman discovered, with a sensation of shock, he was too slow!

Flowing into alignment with great speed, held centrally at waist level in front of the curvaceous feminine torso, the Webley roared as the realization was striking home!

Knowing she had no other choice, if she wanted to survive, Madam shot for an instant kill. Being at a distance which precluded the need to take aim along the stubby barrel, the .450 Eley calibre bullet flew to where it would produce the required effect. Entering the centre of Norman's forehead, the lead brought the

2. *As we describe in:* Part Eleven, the Rockabye County series, 'Preventive Law Enforcement', J.T.'S HUNDREDTH, *modern peace officers indulge in such practice when changing from carrying a handgun in a shoulder holster to a rig on the waist belt or vice versa. J.T.E.*

3. *An example of how dangerous a failure to take such a precaution could prove is recorded in:* THE FAST GUN. *J.T.E.*

148

upwards movement of his revolver to an immediate end.

A startled profanity burst from Lang as he watched his companion going down without so much as getting off a shot. Despite the evidence he had received on their last meeting, he had felt sure the blonde only carried the revolver for show. He had also assumed, the speed with which she had drawn it from the shoulder holster to menace Wallace notwithstanding, she would lack the nerve to do so in a face to face confrontation with an armed adversary. Appreciating just how wrong he had been, he was equally aware that he must now take some action against her. Not to avenge Norman, but—knowing even County Sheriff Lloyd Bowman could do nothing to help him under the circumstances—to save himself from the consequences of what they had planned.

Feeling the hand loosen its grip and the revolver being removed from against her torso, Sally saw and took the chance she was being offered. Snatching free her arm, she sprang away from her captor. While doing so, she hoped her boss would be able to cope with whatever he was planning.

Even before she saw the girl escape, Madam was already setting about preparations to meet the second threat to her life. Relieved by the sight, as it removed the need to have to consider Sally's safety before taking action, she threw herself down in a diving roll. Nor did she move a moment too soon. Even as she was landing on the floor, the Colt in Lang's hand bellowed. Passing so close it clipped plumes from the spray of red dyed ibis feathers in her hair, his bullet did no more than kick up splinters from the planks beyond her. Halting on her stomach, her left hand joining the right on the butt and thumbs cocking the hammer, she fired in echo of the shot.

And missed!

However, except when the hammer was being fanned, an uncocked revolver with a self cocking

149

double action was faster to use than one requiring this necessary function to be performed manually!

Twice more in very rapid succession, the blonde squeezed the trigger and the hammer was taken through its operating cycle. Both bullets tore into the chest of the hard-case, the first arriving an instant before he could manually cock and use his Colt. Thrown from his feet by the double impact, the revolver left his hand and he sprawled limply on to the floor. Although his body moved spasmodically, his companion lying in a loose and uncaring fashion, not too far away, was absolutely still.

Coming to her feet, holding the smoking Webley ready in case it might be needed again, one glance at each man informed Madam the precaution was unnecessary. Oblivious of the excited chatter which arose all around her, she nodded gratitude to the pale faced Sally. Then she swung her gaze to where Aloysius P. Scrope and the other prominent businessmen were hurrying towards her. Before they arrived, her attention having been attracted by seeing three figures bursting through the front entrance—two holding firearms in positions of readiness—she decided the presence of her attorney might prove beneficial. For all that the others were carrying, respectively, a Remington New Army Model of 1863 revolver and a short barrelled ten gauge Greener shotgun, it was the unarmed member of the trio who had led her to draw that conclusion. Making a deduction from the badge of office he was wearing which was different to those displayed by his companions, and remembering comments she had heard about him, added to her assumptions with respect to the purpose of the two hard-cases, she felt she was not doing him an injustice in her estimation of why he had come.

Walking just a little behind Town Marshal Tune Collier and Deputy Town Marshal Herman 'Pocket' Hoscroft, although technically their superior in office, County Sheriff Lloyd Bowman struck Madam as re-

150

sembling Joshua Gilmore apart from having better taste in clothes. Tall, well built, albeit running to seed, already traces of dissipation were beginning to mar his handsome features. It may have been for this reason he had elected to grow Dundreary whiskers, streaked with grey, as was his longish brown hair. He was well dressed in expensive city style clothes. However, while he wore a gunbelt with an ivory handled Colt Navy Model of 1862 revolver in its holster, he did not give the impression of being a fighting man. Nor was he, holding his office more by influence and pliancy where such served his purpose, rather than through any aptitude for law enforcement duties.

'Looks like you've run into a mite of trouble, Madam,' Collier commented, returning the Remington to its cross draw holster on the left side of his gunbelt.

'You could say that, Tune,' the blonde admitted.

'What happened?' Bowman demanded, pushing forward when satisfied it was safe for him to do so.

'I see the mayor's let you take on a new *deputy*, Tune,' Madam remarked, then gave a gasp of what appeared to be embarassment. 'Land's sakes, what a silly *mistake*. That isn't a *deputy's* badge at all!'

'It isn't,' Collier confirmed, poker faced despite the amusement he was feeling. 'This's the sheriff of Sand County, Madam. Lloyd, this's the *lady* I've been telling you about, Madam Bulldog. Madam, allow me to present Lloyd Bowman.'

'*Charmed*,' the blonde responded and contrived to sound as if she almost meant it. Then, gazing around, she went on in a louder voice, 'All right, fellers, it's all over. Now how's about starting spending some money, huh?' Waiting until the suggestion was acted upon by most of the customers, she turned back to the marshal. 'Like you said, Tune, I've run into a mite of trouble.'

'I'll handle things, *marshal*!' Bowman asserted, before the senior municipal peace officer could speak.

'It's your privilege, *sheriff*,' Collier conceded, puzzled

by the unexpected eagerness to attend to duty being displayed by his superior.

'Tell me what happened!' Bowman demanded of the blonde, rather than merely asked.

'You know my attorney, Counsellor Scrope?' Madam inquired, annoyed by the tone in which she had been addressed.

'Of course I d—!' the sheriff began, his manner implying he had no liking for the lawyer. Then he noticed for the first time that the man in question was standing within hearing distance and he nodded a grudging greeting. 'Ah, Scrope, I didn't see you!'

'Good evening,' the attorney replied. 'Can I be of any *assistance*, Madam Bulldog?'

'I don't reckon so, Counsellor,' the blonde replied.

'I'll be around if you need me,' Scrope promised, but the words had more of the timbre of a threat.

'Now, what were you saying, *sheriff*?' Madam inquired.

'Do you mind telling me what happened?' Bowman requested, his manner less hectoring as he saw the quality of the group around the attorney, none of whom showed any sign of withdrawing. Always more politician than peace officer, thinking of the forthcoming changes in the administration of the State, he was wary of antagonizing men capable of having a detrimental effect upon his career. 'I have to establish the facts, you know.'

'Sure,' Madam agreed, despite believing he had had another reason for arriving. 'I had to shoot those two to stop them shooting me. Which I know you can't take just my word, so ask anybody else you've a mind how they saw it.'

'I certainly can't find any fault in how you acted, ma'am,' the sheriff declared, after having listened to a number of witnesses confirming the assertion that the blonde had behaved in the only manner possible to save her life. He had also heard the reason given by the two hard-cases before trying to kill her. Looking at

152

Doctor Henry Connel, who had arrived during the questioning and was kneeling alongside Lang, he asked, 'Can he speak?'

'Not now and maybe never again,' the medical practitioner replied. 'Shall I let you know if there's a chance of him being able to?'

'You may as well,' Bowman confirmed, seeming less disappointed by the information than might have been expected. 'But I'll be heading back to Garnett early tomorrow morning and that brings up something else. I always make it a rule to look over the gambling gear of the saloons in my bailiwick—Just to be able to say it's all right if somebody claims they was cheated——!'

'Good thinking!' Madam praised, the last part of the comment being directed her way.

'Thank you,' the sheriff answered, looking relieved. 'And, as my stay's of necessity brief, perhaps I could do so while I'm here. Unless it will *inconvenience* you, that is.'

'Go to it in good health,' the blonde offered, having seen Collier give a quick shake of his head, which she took to indicate such inspections were not the regular policy of the peace officer from Garnett. 'Come on, I'll show you everything you want to see.'

Nodding to the marshal and giving a wink with the eye furthest from the sheriff, Madam followed him across the bar-room. Although he glanced at the game of *vingt-un* and a couple of tables at which poker was being played, he led the way straight to the faro layout. Going to where Abel Fletcher was acting as dealer, he watched a few cards being played. Then, acting in a nonchalant fashion which was nearly convincing, he reached to press the switch disguised as a knot in the wood. Nothing happened and, frowning, he jabbed twice more.

'This isn't *my* table,' Madam remarked, giving no sign of having seen what was being done. 'It belongs to Leo Wallace, or *Mrs.* Higgins, and I wish they would

153

send me the one they traded it for, so I can get this back to them. You'll *never* guess what I found?'

'What was it?'

'There's a well hidden drawer in the front and it had a couple of second dealer boxes in it—Happen you know what *they* are?'

'I know what they are!'

'There were two of them and some marked decks of cards,' Madam went on. 'Maybe it was wrong of me, seeing they weren't *mine*, but I had them all burned and got the drawer fixed with glue so it can't be opened.'

'That was good thinking!' Bowman claimed, but with little sincerity, then glanced to where another form of gambling was in progress.

'There were only slick cups for the dice games,' the blonde claimed, looking in the same direction and guessing what he was thinking. 'But I've had their insides roughened and, even if I hadn't burned all the loaded dice *Wallace* left behind, they couldn't be used to rook the customers. Would you like to look them and the dice over?'

'Shucks, no!' Bowman refused, with a jollity he was far from feeling. He felt sure the dishonest leather cups had been treated as was described.[4] In which case, even if loaded dice were used, their effect would be nullified by the roughened interior. Conceding defeat on all the points he had been told by Wanda Higgins

4. *Although an honest leather dice cup has ridges, or is roughened, on the inside, the interior of a 'slick' cup is completely smooth. When using the device and loaded dice, the cheat moves it in a rotary action and not by shaking it as is done in fair play. Therefore, instead of being rattled at random inside the cup, the dice pass around it until centrifugal force causes the numbers for which they are loaded to be uppermost. The dice are then sent from the cup in a sliding motion rather than by being tipped out to fall indiscriminately. J.T.E.*

would be available, he continued, 'I'm satisfied every-thing's run fairly in here.'

'Would you like to join the Counsellor's party and me in a few hands of poker?' Madam invited, with something in her manner appearing to suggest there might be more to the offer than just a game of cards.

'Er, not tonight if you'll excuse me,' the sheriff refused, after a few seconds of temptation. Like the blacksmith, he believed he was irresistible to members of the opposite sex and was generally willing to make the most of such an opportunity as, his ego suggested, he had been offered. However, he realized news of anything of that kind would be sure to reach Wanda Higgins, and she knew far too much about various of his illicit activities for him to dare to antagonize her. 'I still have to finish the rounds with the marshal and I need to make an early start in the morning. So, if you'll excuse me, we'll be on our way.'

'Go ahead,' Madam authorized. 'Are you going by the Barnhof?'

'I was—!' Bowman began.

'Sure we are,' Collier put in, face devoid of any expression, although he was inwardly delighted by the chance with which he had been presented. 'The sheriff wants to go over Rudy Schanz's gambling gear while he's up here. Can we do something for you there?'

'If Moses Stern's there, ask him to get word to his sister that I'd like to have the faro table changed,' Madam replied. 'Maybe she—Leo Wallace will have need for that secret drawer in it.'

'We'll give him the word,' the marshal promised. 'And, seeing I'll be off duty when we've done the rounds, I'll drop by and sit in on that poker game if you don't mind.'

'Feel free,' the blonde agreed. 'One way and another, I've been real lucky tonight. Only I won't be staying late. I'm expecting the wagon with my gear arriving tomorrow and I figured I'd ride out to meet it.'

CHAPTER FOURTEEN

I Want Some Questions Answered

'Good afternoon, Miz Charlie,' Greta Kusin said, showing pleasure, as she walked up to the newly arrived buggy. It had come to a halt a short distance from where the wagon in which she was travelling was standing, its team unhitched. Like her yellowish hair and features, her accent was indicative of Nordic origins. Big and massively built, yet far from flabbily fat, she was clad in a poke bonnet and a gingham dress instead of the maid's uniform generally worn while performing her duties. 'I hope you don't mind, but Vic and me've told those two young cowboys they can stop and eat with us.'

'I don't mind at all,' Madam Bulldog replied, glancing at the men in question. 'But don't start calling me "Miz Charlie" around Tennyson. Apart from Counselor Scrope, he's my attorney, nobody knows I'm Charlotte Canary there.'[1]

'I remember good,' the maid promised. 'Don't you worry 'bout that.'

After having accompanied County Sheriff Lloyd Bowman on the rounds the previous evening, Town

---

1. *Neither the source from which we originally worked, nor the more extensive information supplied by Andrew Mark 'Big Andy' Counter, offer any suggestion of why Charlotte Canary elected to be known only as 'Madam Bulldog'. J.T.E.*

Marshal Tune Collier and Deputy Marshal Herman 'Pockets' Hoscroft had returned to the Hide And Horn Saloon without him. As promised, they had joined the poker game which lasted until almost midnight.

While playing, the blonde had heard enough comments to indicate that the men at her table were surprised by the zeal with which the peace officer from the county seat had performed his duties. It was his responsibility to investigate the shooting, but none had expected him to do so. Much to the amusement of his audience, the elderly deputy had described with relish how he and his immediate superior had turned a deaf ear to suggestions that the visit to, and inspection of, the gambling games at the Barnhof Saloon should be forgotten. He had been equally droll when telling of the consternation caused by the latter. Although Bowman had looked at the games and announced everything met with his approval, Hoscroft had claimed this did not necessarily mean the gambling was being run honestly.

Inviting Collier and Aloysius P. Scrope to her downstairs office at the conclusion of the game, Hoscroft having returned to the jailhouse as he was on overnight duty there, Madam had told them of her suspicions with regards to the arrival of the two hardcases. They had agreed that it was possible the pair had been sent by Wanda Higgins and Leo Wallace, relying upon the 'fortuitous' presence of the county sheriff in Tennyson to evade the consequences. However, the marshal had asserted that proving such a connection existed would be practically impossible. Barry Norman had been killed outright and Herbert Lang died of his wounds without even having regained consciousness. Because Bowman was probably an accessory before the fact and had other, even more serious, activities which could be exposed in return, it was unlikely he could be induced or forced to confess. Acceding to the latter point, the blonde had explained why she made the invitation to join the poker game in such a seemingly promising fashion. The reasons she had drawn with regards to the refusal, a fear of betrayal by Wanda Higgins were—although unproven—accurate.

Putting the matter from her mind after the men had left, Madam had retired for the night. With her morning exercises completed, and having enjoyed her usual hearty breakfast, she had boarded the buggy rented for her by the swamper, Sonny, from Pegler's livery barn and set off alone to meet the wagon in which her maid and cook were bringing the remainder of her property. She had had no difficulty finding them. Following the trail by which she had travelled on the stagecoach from Fort Worth, she had come upon them halted by a stream in a clearing of the wooded country through which they had been passing.

Two good quality cow ponies, a black and a roan, were hobbled and grazing near the wagon's heavier four horse team. Their saddles, low horned and double girthed in the style of Texas, lay—each on its side—where unlikely to come to harm from a careless person treading on them. Identically loaded, there was a coiled lariat strapped to the horn, a bulky tarpaulin-wrapped bed roll attached to the cantle and, butt pointing rearwards, a Winchester Model of 1866 rifle in the boot on the left side.

As she was being greeted by the maid, the blonde studied the owners of the horses and their rigs while preparing to climb down. She concluded neither was likely to require the need for the short barrelled shotgun which she was carrying, to augment the Webley Bulldog revolver in its shoulder holster, beside her on the seat. In their early twenties, their clothing showing signs of having been worn for travelling a good distance, she felt sure they were trustworthy; despite also estimating they could prove themselves quite competent with the weapons carried on their persons.

The taller of the pair was in some respects the more striking. Slender in build, he had black hair and a neatly trimmed moustache. His good looking features suggested a more studious mien than was common amongst cowhands, which his attire implied he was, but the pallor of his face was caused by a resistance to tanning rather than through spending much time indoors. Unlike his companion, who had on the more usual calfskin vest, he was wearing a brown coat with its right side stitched back to leave unimpeded access to the ivory handled Colt Army Model of 1860 revolver in the fast draw holster of a gunbelt produced by an obviously excellent leatherworker.

Lacking two inches of his companion's height, but equally a Texas' cowhand as far as his clothing was concerned, the second young man was broader shouldered and more strongly built. His face was freckled, ruggedly pleasant and cheerful. Although the revolver in his fast draw holster was a walnut handled Dance Army Model, made during the War Between The States for the Confederate forces, he was sufficiently well dressed to suggest this was by personal preference rather than because a lack of funds prevented him from purchasing a more modern handgun.

'Howdy, boys,' Madam greeted, walking forward. 'You headed for Tennyson?'

'Why sure, ma'am, but only passing through,' the taller cowhand replied, his voice suggestive of a good education and, not surprisingly, having a Texan's drawl. 'This here's Rusty Willis and I'm called Doc Leroy.'

'That wasn't what our cook's called him one time, ma'am,' the second product of the cattle business asserted, also in the fashion of one born and raised in the Lone Star State. 'Nor our boss, Stone Hart, more than once.'

'I can guess and reckon it'd be deserved,' the blonde declared with a smile. 'But I'll bet *you* never *ever* gave them call to speak anything but kindly about you.'

159

'If I did, may lightning strike Doc down!' Jason 'Rusty' Willis replied and, after looking upwards expectantly for a moment, went on in an exasperated manner, 'Drat, *He* wasn't *listening*!'

'You'll have to excuse my *amigo*, ma'am,' Marvin Eldridge 'Doc' Leroy requested. 'Trouble is, his momma *didn't* drop him on his head when he was a baby and he's never been the same since. Which most folks say they wish he'd just never been at all. Anyways, we've heard tell the Hide And Horn Saloon down to Tennyson's got a new owner—!'

'And you know you're talking to her,' the blonde interrupted with a smile. 'Are all the Wedge crew like you pair?'

'Heaven forbid they should be so *lucky*, ma'am!' Rusty answered, concluding the buxom newcomer had a fair knowledge of the cattle business to be aware of the outfit for which he and his companion rode.[2] 'Fact being, 'cepting Stone Hart—him being the *boss* and me a loyal apple polisher—they're *worse*.'

'I'm damned if I can see how that's *possible*!' Madam claimed, knowing enough about cowhands to feel sure such banter would be appreciated by the two young men; of whom—at least in the case of the taller—she had heard on more than one occasion. 'Did you know I've got a good friend of yours dropping by around the middle of the week, Doc?'

'Who'd that be, ma'am?'

'Joe Brambile.'

'*Bueno*!' Doc enthused. 'I haven't run across good ole Joe in a coon's age.'

'Maybe he'll've run across Hayden Lindrick, *amigo*,' Rusty suggested and all the levity had left him.

2. *Information regarding some of the activities of the Wedge crew—who acted as contract trail hands for ranchers with too samll a number of stock, to make up and deliver a herd of their own to the Kansas shipping pens—can be found in:* QUIET TOWN, TRIGGER FAST, GUN WIZARD *and* THE RIO HONDO KID *J.T.E.*

'He'd have got word to me if he had,' the taller cowhand stated, losing the cheerful timbre from his voice.

'I've never heard of Den Lindrick since——!' Madam began, being aware of what had caused the change in the attitude of the two young men. Letting the words trail off, she decided against saying she found it hard to believe the person they were discussing had committed the heinous crime for which Doc was clearly still hoping to take revenge. Instead, she went on, 'Anyways, the grub's ready and waiting. If you boys aren't starving, we'll start into it as soon as I've been to look for butterflies in the bushes.'

Strolling into the woodland, although feeling certain neither of the cowhands was the kind to follow and watch her, the blonde went a short distance before locating what she considered to be a suitable spot for her needs. Removing her jacket, she peeled off the shoulder holster and hung it over the branch of a towering dogwood bush, where it would be within easy reaching distance, before unfastening the waist band of her skirt. Again, the precaution was not taken against the possibility of finding herself spied upon by one or both Texans. She was aware that rattlesnakes, among other dangerous creatures, frequented such terrain and wanted to be able to protect herself while in the vulnerable position created by her present needs.

While squatting behind the bushes, answering the call of nature, Madam heard horses. However, the sound caused her no concern. She estimated they were coming along the trail she had used. There were many innocuous reasons for riders to be in the vicinity, such as cowhands returning belatedly to their ranch after having spent Saturday night celebrating in Tennyson, so she did not bother to hurry. After she had adjusted her nether garments, judging that the newcomers would soon be in sight of where the wagon was stationed, she replaced her shoulder holster and, donning her jacket, made her way back to the wagon.

161

Standing by the fire with cups of coffee in their hands, Doc Leroy and Rusty Willis were waiting for the blonde to return before commencing their meal. They too had had their attention attracted by the sound of hooves. Being in a better position, they were soon able to see the five men who were coming at a leisurely pace along the trail from Tennyson. Studying the middle sized and over weight professional gambler in the lead, they turned their gaze next to the lanky, poorly dressed town dweller by his side. Neither struck them as the kind to be accompanied by the other three riders. Unless their range-wise eyes were at fault, they figured the trio to be small town hardcases of the sort willing to do anything for money except sweat-raising work or taking chances. However, knowing their own competence at matters *pistolero* and being unacquainted with recent events in the town from which the quintet had come, neither cowhand saw any reason to be worried by the new arrivals.

'Hello the fire!' the gambler called, bringing his companions to a halt, as was required by range country etiquette, although they were traversing a public trail. 'Do you have any coffee and chow to spare?'

'We're long on coffee,' replied the small, cheerful but no longer young man who acted as cook and general handyman for Madam Bulldog. 'But, seeing's we wasn't expecting company, we won't have enough food for you.'

'Coffee'll do us fine,' Matthew McDonald declared swinging from his saddle. 'Come on, boys. Let's have ourselves a cup afore we ride on.'

Having made good their escape from the Hide And Horn Saloon after the failure of their first attempt to cheat the new owner, the gambler and Samuel Shardlow had taken refuge in the room the latter rented at a cheap hotel. They had expected to be sought, either by the marshal or by members of the blonde's staff, bu

162

neither eventuality had happened. Nevertheless, knowing they could not count upon any of Joshua Gilmore's crowd for support, they had concluded a change of scenery was advisable.

Remembering that the woman responsible for their downfall was expecting a wagon loaded with unspecified property to come from Fort Worth, the pair had seen a chance of taking a profitable revenge. Selecting the three hard-cases to assist them, they had contrived to discover when the shipment was expected to reach Tennyson and had set out to intercept it. On hearing from the man they had sent ahead as scout that there were two cowhands with the couple bringing the wagon, there had been some argument over what to do. Pointing out that neither the man and woman or the cowhands had any reason to expect trouble, particularly when so close to their destination, McDonald had proposed a scheme which met with the approval of the others. Satisfied that the odds were still in their favour, particularly as the gambler's scheme should provide them with the vital element of surprise, they had ridden on as a single group and were about to put their plan into effect.

On the surface, the plan proposed by McDonald was excellent!

However, unbeknown to any of the quintet, there were two doubtful factors which had not been anticipated!

In the first place, not liking the look of the hard-cases in particular, the cowhands were far more alert than they appeared on the surface!

Secondly and of far greater importance, the gambler had not realized there was somebody in the vicinity who knew him and would be even more doubtful of his motives!

'McDonald!'

Hearing his name called and seeing who was coming through the trees, the gambler did not wait to find out what was intended. Giving a yell of, 'Get the bastards!' he grabbed for the revolver tucked into the silk sash about his midsection. With their nerves already on edge, the situation having developed a more dangerous trend than was envisaged when it was planned, the rest of the newcomers duplicated his action and began to reach for their weapons.

Starting to draw her Webley with all the speed she could muster, Madam Bulldog discovered, from the corner of her eye, that, the two young Texans were responding in a satisfactory manner!

Allowing the cup to fall from his grasp, Doc Leroy was the fastest of everybody involved. Even before it landed at his feet, his seemingly boneless right hand was making a white flash of movement. So swiftly did the Colt leave the specially designed holster that, as his fingers and thumb enfolded the ivory handle in their grasp, it seemed that his hand and the gun met in mid-air. Although the revolver spoke at waist level, the .44 calibre soft lead ball took McDonald in the centre of the chest before his own weapon had cleared his sash.

The blonde was second into action, beating Rusty by a smaller margin than if she too had elected to employ instinctive alignment. Having a greater distance between herself and the newcomers, she took the fractionally longer time to adopt a double handed and eye level posture. Firing twice, the second bullet took Shardlow in the head. Coming an instant later, the first lead discharged by the shorter cowhand proved that the Dance was still a useful weapon in competent hands by tumbling the fastest moving of the hardcases with a wound in the thigh. Not, unfortunately, before he was able to shoot and, missing his target, which was Doc, he hit the elderly cook in the right side of the chest.

Despite having started their draws, neither of the surviving men brought them to completion. Instead, they turned with flight in mind. Their movements were giving an added stimulus to rapidity. The horses which had been left ground hitched by dangling reins, as was customary in range country, were showing alarm at the disturbance. Although normally they would have stood still, they were beginning to turn away from the commotion with the intention of bolting. Dashing up, each of the remaining hard-cases contrived to catch hold of reins and a saddlehorn. They made flying mounts which produced the desired effect. Once afork their captured mounts, expecting to be fired at and perhaps hit, they gave all their attention to putting as much distance between themselves and their intended victims as quickly as possible.

'Seems like you knew the gambling m——!' Doc began, looking from the victims of the fight to Madam Bulldog.

'Oh my God!' the maid screamed, bringing the words to a halt. 'Vic's *hit*!'

'God damn it!' the blonde ejaculated, hurrying towards the fire as she returned the Webley to its holster. Looking for a moment at the wound, she heard footsteps approaching and swung her head around to see who was coming, saying, 'This looks *bad*!'

'It doesn't just *look* bad, ma'am,' corrected the pallid faced Texan, gazing down. 'It *is* bad. *Real* bad!'

'Will either you or Rusty saddle up and head for Tennyson to fetch Doctor Connel?' Madam requested.

'There's no time for that,' Doc stated. 'Open up my bed roll and get my bag out *pronto*, Rusty!'

'Yo!' assented the shorter cowhand and hurried towards the saddles.

'Of *course*!' the blonde gasped, remembering something which she had forgotten in her concern for the welfare of the injured man at her feet. 'Just how much is there to all those tales going around about you doctoring folks?'

'I've not qualified as a M.D., if that's what you mean, although I hope to one day,'[3] Doc replied, holstering

---

3. *How the ambition to qualify as a Doctor of Medicine was*

his Colt and removing the black Texas style Stetson hat from where it was dangling by its *barbiquejo* on his back. 'And I used something a touch more medical than Silent Churchman's bowie knife, and a hit over the head with an empty whiskey bottle, when I had to take out Peaceful Gunn's appendix in the Indian Nations. But I keep in touch with what's doing in the doctoring world and one thing I've had plenty of chance to work on is bullet wounds.'

'It's not that I—!' Madam began.

'I know, ma'am,' the slender Texan drawled. 'And count on me to do the best I can for this gent. Greta can help me and, while we're 'tending to Vic, maybe you and Rusty'd best see to those three yahoos we downed. Way he's taking on over there, at least one of them's still alive and hurting.'

'Leave him to us!' the blonde confirmed grimly, wanting to interrogate any survivors and discover whether Wanda Higgins was behind the attempted robbery. 'I want some questions answered and, if it's the only way I can get them, I'll tell him you'll leave him to bleed to death unless he talks.'

'You do that, ma'am,' Doc agreed, taking off his jacket and looking to where his *amigo* was already removing the black medical bag which was always the uppermost item in his war bag. 'God damn it, though, *this* always happens!'

'What?' Madam inquired.

'Every time I get into a shooting scrape away from a town,' the pallid faced Texan replied. 'I wind up having to patch up at least one of the sons-of-bitches who were trying to gun me down!'

achieved and the connection between Marvin Eldridge 'Doc' Leroy and Hayden Lindrick, is described in: DOC LEROY, M.D. J.T.E

CHAPTER FIFTEEN

Find Out Who's The Better Woman

Dancing as if in a pagan ritual, while throwing hooks, jabs and cross hits against the specially designed, straw filled punching bag, Wanda Higgins was somewhat more adequately dressed than on the last occasion in Tennyson when she had used it for training and to relieve her angry feelings. However, due to the strenuous exercises she had already been engaged in, the thin white cotton, sleeveless man's undershirt, the black tights and white pumps, were so saturated, the effect was as though she was bare to the waist. She was completely oblivious of this. Nor, despite being subjected to a lascivious scrutiny by two men, would she have felt perturbed, or embarrassed, if she had realised they were staring at her. Instead, she continued to assail the bag, as it moved under the impulsion of her gloved fists, with a savage vigour neither had seen her come close to exhibiting during her previous training sessions.

In the light of recent events, the red head considered she now had an even more vitally important reason to improve her ability in such an unfeminine activity!

Having left the house at Tennyson in the fashion she had selected, Wanda and her half-brother had hoped their absence would only need to be of sufficient length to supply them with an alibi. Taking up what they had expected to be only a temporary residence in Garnett, they had set about making arrangements for their return and reclaim of the Hide And Horn Saloon. On being consulted, Counselor Otis J. Grimsdyke had claimed this might be possible if the present owner had not made a will and died intestate. Following the plan they had thought up, Leo Wallace had 'refused' to give pay to Barry Norman and Herbert Lang when 'confronted' by them in the County Seat Saloon. 'Reprisals' against him were 'prevented' by the presence of County Sheriff Lloyd Bowman and they had left claiming in loud voices that they intended to collect the money owed them from the woman they blamed for having been fired from the saloon.

Even before hearing that the proposed killing of Madam Bulldog had failed, the red head had continued her rigorous exercise and training programme. In anticipation of regaining control of the business lost by her husband, she wanted to be ready to take the revenge she was planning against Viola Grant. Learning that the buxom blonde for whom she had developed an even greater hatred than was directed against the saloon-girl—had survived the murder attempt, she had found a new purpose to drive her into extra effort so as to acquire added fitness and skill.

Watching the voluptuous red head working out on Wednesday morning, displaying an interest which went beyond merely wishing to form an estimation of her ability, were Wallace and the trainer supplied by the sheriff.

Short, thin, rat-faced, badly shaven and balding, Stephen Good was an even less imposing figure than the gambler. He was wearing a flat cap so grimy as to render its original colour indistinguishable, a grubby white woollen turtleneck sweater, Levi pants which had to have seen better days, and filthy Pawnee moccasins. Despite his undoubted skill as a trainer, he did not live up to his name. He had, in fact, 'gone to Texas' as a result of a scandal involving thrown fight and the use of illicit methods he had taught to the

168

boxers in his charge. Having no desire to be arrested and returned to the East, where several less than scrupulous followers of the fistic sport were eager to lay hands upon him, he had been more than willing to accept the task of training the red head, when it was offered by the sheriff, than might otherwise have proved the case. Agreeable as he had considered the prospect of being able to watch the scantily dressed and voluptuous woman, even to handle her body as part of his duties, he had been less enamoured of the realization that he would be staying in one spot for a longer period than he cared for. A combination of the threat of extradition and a promise of protection had brought him to an amenable frame of mind. Although the matter was never raised, he had found the task enjoyable and, as yet, had had no cause to regret having been compelled to take it on.

'Well,' the gambler asked, forcing himself to think of something other than what was running through his mind as he feasted his eyes upon the well defined curves of his half-sister's body. 'What do you reckon to her, Stevie?'

'She's good,' replied the trainer, his voice that of a New Yorker from one of the less salubrious districts, also turning his thoughts from the kind of bed-mate the red head might make. 'In fact, I reckon we could make a helluva lot of money taking her on a tour of saloons and theatres and such.'

'How'd she be in a real fight, though?' Wallace inquired, knowing Wanda would be unlikely to even consider such a proposal while there was still a chance of once more taking possession of the Hide And Horn Saloon.

'She'd have a better than fair chance of winning,' Good estimated. Thinking of the occasions he had sparred with the red head, he went on, 'She hits hard and has a mean streak which'll stop her worrying over how bad she'll be hurting whoever she's punching. With what I've taught her, she shouldn't have no trouble at all in beating the shit out of a saloon gal who don't know nothing 'cept hair yanking.'

'How'd she be against this Madam Bulldog's slickered Maxie out of the Hide?' the gambler wanted to know. 'What I've heard, she's real handy with her dukes.'

'Is, huh?'

'She put Moe Stern down so hard he thought she'd gutted him.'

'That don't mean she's *good*,' the trainer sniffed. 'One hard 'n' in that lard and liquor filled gut and he'd go down like he was boned.

'She took out Vi Grant and two more of the gals,' Wallace stated. 'And, from what I've heard, put down Matt McDonald. Which sounds to me like she's good with her dukes. So how will Wan' stack up against her?'

'I couldn't say, not having seen her using her dukes,' Good claimed, keeping his attention on the red head. 'But Wanda's as good as any fister I've handled. Is she aiming to take on this Madam Bulldog instead of the saloon gal?'

'I don't know what she's aiming to do,' the gambler admitted, showing just a trace of the annoyance he felt over the way in which his half-sister kept him in ignorance of her intentions. 'All I know is, she's going at this training harder than she used to before she met Madam Bulldog in Lawyer Scrope's office.'

Before any more could be said, the door of the room to which the simply equipped gymnasium had been transferred was opened. Neither Wallace nor Good showed any surprise on seeing Sheriff Bowman come in. As owner of the building, although he lived in a suite at the best hotel Garnett could offer, he had the right of access at all times.

'Wanda!' the peace officer boomed, closing the door and walking forward without so much as a nod to acknowledge the presence of the other two men who

170

were also present. 'Hey, Wanda. Stop for a moment, will you?'

'Well?' the red head asked, after having delivered two rapid jabs to the facial area, followed by a punch to the side of the bag's 'head' which would have felled any human being receiving it. Moving away, her bosom rising and falling as she sucked in deep breaths to replenish her lungs, she went on, 'What is it?'

'I've just come from the stage depot,' Bowman announced, keeping his eyes on the sight presented by the still heavily breathing woman. 'You'll *never* guess who got dropped off by the coach at Tennyson.'

'And I'm in no mood to even *try!*' Wanda said shortly. 'I've been working out like a god-damned nigger ever since I got up!'

'Who was it?' Wallace asked, feeling sure the disembarking passengers must be .of importance to have aroused such a display of interest on the part of the peace officer.

'Poker Alice, Joe Brambile and Pappy Maverick,' Bowman named, although a frown had come to his face at the chilling response from the red head. 'It seems they're some of the gambling big wheels who've been invited to sit in on a high stake game Madam Bulldog's going to hold later in the week.'

'I hope they take her for every god-damned thin red dime she's got!' Wallace spat out viciously, knowing he could not have attracted even three such prominent players to join him in a game of any kind.

'Which wouldn't do a thing to help us get the Hide back!' Wanda pointed out sarcastically and held out her hands. 'Here, Stevie, take off the gloves. I've done enough for the time being!'

'Sure, Wan',' the trainer assented. 'You done real good!'

'Good Christ!' Bowman ejaculated, staring at the bandages around the hands which were exposed by the removal of the gloves. 'Have you hurt yourself?'

'Of course not!' the red head snorted, starting to don

a thick robe without waiting for the white wrapping to be removed. 'They're to help protect my knuckles.'

'Is that *all*?' the sheriff sniffed, disappointed at the concealment of an attire he considered to be more erotically stimulating than the sight of Wanda completely naked. 'Anyways, there's something else.'

'What would that be?' the red head demanded impatiently, when the information was not forthcoming. She found the peace officer's habit of making it necessary to seek an answer more annoying than usual.

'I've just got word from a feller in Austin who owes me favours,' Bowman explained. 'He says Stanton Howard will be here on Thursday.'

'Stanton Howard!' Wanda breathed.

'He's the one most fancied to replace Davis as Governor,' the sheriff explained, electing to treat the words of the red head as a question rather than an exclamation registering interest.

'I know very well who Stanton Howard *is*, thank you!' Wanda snapped, but the sight of annoyance coming to the face of the peace officer struck a warning note. Realizing she would need to retain his support in her planned retrieval of the Hide And Horn Saloon, she forced herself to adopt a more conciliatory tone as she continued, 'I'm sorry, Lloyd. It's all this god-damned exercise making me irritable.'

'I understand, Wan',' the sheriff declared, showing he was mollified by the apology.

'So Stanton Howard's coming here, is he?' the red head said pensively.

'Yes. He's trying to call in on as many towns as possible before he takes office.'

'Is he going to Tennyson?'

'I don't know.'

'Can you persuade him to, if he isn't?'

'*Persuade* him?' Bowman repeated, with no great enthusiasm, thinking of how his supporters in Garnet

172

might regard such behaviour on his part. 'Why should I do that?'

'For *me*!' Wanda purred rather than merely replied.

'Will having him go there help you to get back the Hide?' the sheriff asked, the two words having been charged with the kind of promise which past experience had taught him was of a most satisfying nature.

'It could help,' the red head claimed. 'Bulldog's been riling some folks, Moe's sent word to tell me. They didn't take kindly to her gunning down Norman and Lang, even though it was in self defence, and're less happy now she's made wolf bait out of McDonald and two fellers she reckons were figuring on stealing a wagon load of her gear. They say so much killing's going to get the town a bad name.'

'And so it is, by god!' the sheriff asserted, but his response was not caused by any sense of responsibility for the maintaining of law and order throughout Sand County. Not only did he find the possibility of violence satisfying, as it could have an adverse effect upon a claim for the transference of the status of county seat to Tennyson, but he believed such an attitude would further ingratiate himself with the beautiful and, when in the mood, sexually forthcoming woman. 'And I can't say that I'm any too pleased to have her shooting up my bailiwick, comes to that.'

'Yes, Moe says she's getting real unpopular in some circles,' Wanda commented, showing no sign of having ever heard Bowman's declaration, much less been impressed by it. 'And I aim to make her even more unpopular.'

'How?' the sheriff asked and the other two men showed an equal interest.

'By having damned near every man in town watching her instead of waiting to meet Stanton Howard when he arrives,' the red head replied, extending and gesturing with her hands to Good. As he was removing the bandages, she explained what she had in mind

173

and finished, 'Can you be sure to get him there on Friday afternoon just before four, Lloyd?'

'I believe I can,' Bowman replied. 'He'll be wanting to meet as many people as he can and, as I'm willing to bet he knows about those bastards in Tennyson wanting to become the county seat, he'll probably be meaning to go anyhow.'

'Will *you* make sure he comes?' Wanda demanded.

'If it's mortally possible, I will!' the sheriff promised. 'But aren't you taking a big chance?'

'Not if Stevie's as good as he's told me he is,' the red head stated with confidence. 'In fact, could be I'll have to take things easy so it'll last long enough for what I want to happen.'

* * *

'Regardless of what I thought, that Higgins chappie wasn't exaggerating after all, Charlie,' declared the shapely, beautiful, blonde and elegantly dressed Englishwoman who went by the name, 'Poker Alice', as she looked around the main bar-room of the Hide And Horn Saloon with approval. Although she and the two men with whom she had entered had arrived in Tennyson the previous morning, they had delayed paying a visit to their intended hostess in a high stake poker game until just after sundown on Wednesday. 'This is quite impressive, darling.'

'It is,' Madam Bulldog agreed, her manner expressing a friendliness which matched that of the three distinguished visitors. 'And I hope you and Madame Moustache keep that in mind when you come together.'

'My dear, *that* was all in the past and we really are good friends now,' Poker Alice replied, thinking of her first meeting with the other lady gambler and the fight which had ensued, as she knew it was to this that the buxom blonde was referring. 'Oh, by the by, do you know the owner of the Fortescue Hotel?'

174

'He's a friend of mine,' Madam confirmed, hoping there was no complaint about the accommodation and service.

'Don't look so *alarmed*, darling, it's a charming place,' Poker Alice reassured. 'But you might *suggest* he hires some bell-boys. Why it almost seemed I would have to carry my bags to my room.'[1]

The exercise would have done you good,' Madam claimed with a smile. 'Except, knowing *you*, I'd bet you didn't wind up having to.'

'And you'd be right, dear lady,' asserted Joseph Brambile. Tall, slender, handsome, although no longer young, he dressed like a very successful Southern plantation owner from the days when cotton was king. 'Miz Alice had every man in the place close to fighting for the *right*, privilege even, of helping her.'

'There were so many of them so eager, Joe and I got most of ours toted up along of Alice's,' went on Abraham "Pappy" Maverick, who was tall, sturdily build, white haired and clad in the fashion of a prosperous professional gambler. 'What's the chance of finding some *action* around town, Charlie-gal?'

'Action, Pappy?' Madam queried.

'Don't tell me to try the Barnhof, *please*,' Maverick requested. 'I was in there last night and it was so easy taking that bunch I was up against, it was all I could do to keep awake at the table.'

'You could try the Longhorn,' the buxom blonde suggested, it being considered courtesy for those playing in the kind of game she intended to run to avoid competing against one another until the session commenced. 'But I don't think you'll find anybody much better down there. Anyways, it's great to see you all and I'm looking forward to getting sat around a table ag——!'

'Is something wrong?' Poker Alice inquired, as her

---

1. *The suggestion was acted upon, as we point out in:* CUT ONE, THEY ALL BLEED. *J.T.E.*

hostess brought the comment to a halt and stared at the main entrance. Turning her gaze in the same direction, she studied the group of people who were entering and went on, 'Is she an *entertainer* you've hired along with her admirers, Charlie, or are they a delegation?'

'She's not an entertainer, but they could be a delegation,' Madam replied, wondering what had brought the wife of the former owner, Leo Wallace, Moses Stern, Joshua Gilmore and several of his cronies from the 'sporting' crowd to the Hide And Horn Saloon. Her questioning of the wounded would-be robber had failed to establish any connections with the red head and she was inclined to believe she was in error suspecting complicity from that direction. 'But I reckon we'll soon find out!'

'Is it going to be of a *private* nature?' Brambile asked, unbuttoning his jacket to offer unimpeded access to the revolver carried in a spring retention shoulder holster on his left side.

'Not as far as the red haired *lady* is concerned,' Maverick commented, right hand making what appeared to be a casual gesture which, nevertheless, moved the flap of his black cutaway coat clear of the ivory butt of his low tied Army Colt.

'In which case, darlings,' Poker Alice continued, allowing the neck of her reticule to open and permit easy admittance of her right hand if the Remington Double Deringer reposing therein should be required. 'I don't think it amiss if we consider it isn't *private* for us, either.'

'Good evening, Mrs. Higgins,' Madam greeted, having advanced a few steps in front of her friends after nodding her gratitude for their promised support. Glancing around as she came to a halt before the red head, she decided there were many other allies present if the need arose. 'And to what do I owe the *honour* of this visit?'

'I don't think Maxie would want you to go on

running the Hide for him, the way you've been gunning men down,' Wanda Higgins replied, speaking in tones calculated to carry all around the room. 'So I've come to tell you to get out.'

'Now why would Maxie care how I run the Hide?' the buxom blonde asked, aware that everybody present was listening to the conversation.

'*Oh come on now!*' the red head scoffed, her manner derisive. 'You and I both know he only sent you here pretending you'd won the Hide from him, so's his *legally married* wife and his kin would leave it all to you and him.'

'*Oh come on now* yourself!' Madam countered, employing a similar tone for the first four words. 'You know you're lying in your teeth when you say that.'

'I'm *what?*'

'Lying in your teeth!'

'God damn it, you lousy fat old whore——!' Wanda screeched. 'I'll——!'

'You'll do *what?*' Madam challenged, making her voice as calm as the words addressed to her had been strident.

Watching and listening to the exchange, Wallace felt a sense of alarm which was shared by Gilmore. Each was all too aware of how quickly the temper of the red head could erupt into physical violence. With that in mind, they were hoping she could keep it under control and achieve the purpose for which they had come. Glancing around, they realized that the blonde could count upon the active support of far more people than they had at their disposal and, should the situation turn hostile, they did not care to contemplate the possible effect upon themselves.

'I know you've been telling everybody how you ran me out of town——!' Wanda began.

'You don't know any such thing,' Madam corrected. 'Now let's both of us cut out this mouth-flapping horse shit and get around to what you're really here for.'

'You told everybody how you called me down in Lawyer Scrope's office and I——!'

'Get to the point, *pronto*, or get the hell out of here!'

'You reckoned then you could beat the hell out of me!'

'Those weren't my exact words. But, comes push for shove, I reckon I can.'

'Is that so?' Wanda cried, delighted at having been presented so easily with the opportunity she required.

'I'm satisfied it's so,' Madam claimed, although puzzled by the way in which the conversation was developing. No matter how low her regard for the red head, she could not believe the intention was to provoke a tooth and claw fight between them. 'Have you a mind to *try* and prove different right *now*?'

'If you mean, am I willing to brawl with you like the common, tail-peddling slut you are,' the red head replied. 'The answer is, "*no*". But, should you have the guts to meet me in the ring at the Barnhof, with *boxing gloves* on, then we'll soon enough find out who's the better woman!'

'In the ring,' the blonde repeated, listening to the rumble of excited comment arising as the suggestion was heard by the other occupants of the room. 'With *boxing gloves*?'

'Does the idea scare you?' Wanda mocked.

'Not particularly. But what do *you* expect to get out of it?'

'*This saloon!*'

'And what're you putting up against *my* saloon?'

'Putting up against it?' the red asked, frowning.

'Your husband put it up against ten thousand of my money when he lost it to me,' Madam explained. 'How about you?'

'I'll put up the same!' Wanda promised. Although she was far from destitute she had nowhere near such a large sum—but she was so confident of victory she wanted to leave no avenue for her intended victim to back out.

'Then I'll take you on,' the blonde declared, knowing there was no other choice open to her after so public a discussion. Having already gained a reputation locally for her toughness, she would be unable to continue running the Hide And Horn Saloon—particularly in the way she envisaged—if she refused. However, suspecting the truth about the red head's financial position, she went on, 'But I want another two thousand dollars to boot.[2] We both bring that much and it's held at the side of the ring. Winner takes it all.'

'All right,' Wanda agreed, after a brief pause for thought. She could afford that share of the purse and felt sure that the blonde's suggestion of having it merely intended to persuade her to withdraw from the fight. 'That'll be just so much more for me to win.'

'Which remains to be seen,' Madam answered. 'Do you want to get at it straight away?'

'Certainly not,' the red head refused. 'For one thing, the ring isn't ready. Unless you show yellow and don't come, we'll meet on Friday afternoon at half past three.'

'Have it your way,' the blonde assented, although wondering why that particular time had been selected. 'Friday, at half past three in the afternoon, it is!'

2. 'To boot': a term, used originally by horse and other traders dealing mainly in barter, for something given over and above the price agreed upon in a transaction. J.T.E.

CHAPTER SIXTEEN

There'll Be A Riot If It's Stopped

'Gentlemen—my apologies—*Ladies* and gentlemen!'
Joshua Gilmore bellowed, making the revision as he
saw Poker Alice and the black haired, beautiful,
equally well dressed, buxom Madame Moustache—
who had arrived in Tennyson that morning—as well as
several saloon-girls in the large crowd gathered
around the boxing ring. Clearly enjoying to the full his
role of introducing the event which had attracted the
attention of everybody in the town and surrounding
area, he went on, 'Presenting, in a bout of fisticuffs! Of
three minute rounds, with a minute recovery time
between each! Lasting until one lady cannot beat a
count of ten! For a purse of four thousand dollars and
ownership of the Hide And Horn Saloon. In the red
corner, WANDA HIGGINS. In the blue corner,
MADAM BULLDOG!'

Having achieved her purpose in persuading the
buxom blonde to meet her in the boxing ring on
Wednesday evening, the red head had left the making
of arrangements for the fight to Leo Wallace and the
blacksmith. Knowing what was expected of them, the
latter having received his instructions when she had
returned from a hurried journey to Garnett, they had
done all they could to ensure there was no way in
which the new owner of the saloon could avoid
participating in the fight. If she should do so, it had

been ascertained she would forfeit it by default. In the latter event, even if she tried to renege on the agreement, public opinion would drive her out of Tennyson.

In addition to stipulating the conditions under which the event was to take place, such as the length of each round and rest period and the only way victory could be attained, the two men had suggested Doctor Henry Connel as referee, due to his being known to have acted in this capacity elsewhere. There had been two reasons for making the, on the surface, unusual appointment. Regardless of being on better terms with Madam than their principal, he could be relied upon to act with complete impartiality; albeit offering the chance to imply favouritism should he have to make judgements on the behaviour of the blonde. Furthermore, while Wanda would have the expert seconding of Stephen Good, it would prevent the blonde from receiving the attention of one who, by virtue of his medical skill, would have served her very well in that duty. Aware of how important such competent attention could be, the conspirators had been confident that Madam would not be seconded by anybody with near the ability of the professional trainer in such vital matters as dealing with cuts and supplying restoratives between the rounds.

Aware of the criticism caused in certain circles by her having to defend herself, to the extent of taking the lives of other human beings, Madam had realized that what she was being compelled to do would be considered as probably even less acceptable behaviour. It was almost certain to spoil whatever improved impression had been formed by the Ladies Guild For Civic Betterment, for example. Therefore, she would have preferred the affair to have received as little publicity outside the saloon as possible. Being a realist, she had felt positive this would not prove to be the case.

In fact, the news was already spreading while the conditions of the bout were being settled!

Shortly after the departure of the conspirators, Town Marshal Tune Collier and Counselor Aloysius P. Scrope had arrived together in what was clearly haste. Asking the blonde to discuss the matter with them in her private office, she had agreed. Once there, they had expressed their concern over the situation in which she had allowed herself to become involved. This had gone beyond the damaging of the good impression she had been creating amongst many of her former critics.

While nothing was known about the participation of Good, the woman hired to clean and cook at the house by Maxwell Higgins also served in the former capacity for the attorney. She had told him of Wanda's activities in the simply equipped gymnasuim, and he had found the description of the specially made punching bag most significant. Knowing she would never take so much trouble merely for the sake of harmless—if health-ensuring—exercise, he had suspected her intentions with regards to Viola Grant. Mentioning this to the peace officer, they had concluded her hatred was now being directed against the woman for whom they had formed a liking and respect.

Admitting everything she had been told was correct, Madam had pointed out the adverse effect a refusal of the challenge would have had upon her. Conceding this was the case, her visitors had repeated the warning of the possible repercussions whether she won or lost. However, on the matter being raised by the marshal, Scrope had asserted there was no legislation to prevent the participation of women in a prize fight and it could not be cancelled on legal grounds.

The declaration by the lawyer had helped Collier to justify his inability to prevent the bout, when visited by an irate delegation from the Ladies Guild For Civic Betterment, as soon as he arrived at the jailhouse on Thursday morning. This had not been the news they hoped for and he was left in no doubt that Madam Bulldog had lost whatever improved feelings she might have developed amongst them by her behaviour up to that day.

However, the marshal had found himself faced with another problem relating to the forthcoming fight!

It too had defied refusal!

Learning that Rudolph Schanz was having the boxing ring taken and erected between the blacksmith's shop and Pegler's livery barn, Collier had gone to find out why this was being done. He was told there was already so much interest aroused that the crowd wishing to attend could not be accomodated in the Barnhof Saloon and the bout was to be held in the open. Accepting that to do otherwise might lead to trouble between those inside the building, and others unable to gain admission, the marshal had also conceded the danger and fire hazard which would be created by packing the building to capacity, even disregarding other contingencies.

Receiving a grudging acquiescence from the peace officer, Schanz had had every man he could persuade working on the erection of stands of seats for the expected crowd. By keeping them at it all day, long into the night and throughout Friday morning, he had achieved his purpose and the precaution had proved justifiable. Despite Collier's hope that inclement weather would cause the cancellation of the fight, the day was fine and not too warm. By three o'clock, every stand was full. Men were also standing on the roof of the blacksmith's shop and in the hay loft of the livery barn.

Watching what was happening from the rear of the assembled throng, the marshal had told Deputy Marshal Herman 'Pockets' Hoscroft there were only two things for which they might be grateful. As yet, everybody was in good spirits and there had been no trouble. Furthermore, the location of the ring ensured nothing happening in it could be seen from the frontage of Vernon Street in general and the Square in particular.

Leaning against the hard turnbuckle of the corner to which she had been assigned, with Wallace and Good waiting to act as her seconds, Wanda Higgins considered she was presenting a sight to please the most demanding male member of the audience. She was clad in a white satin version of the man's undershirt, except it was far more daring in cut and showed all too clearly there was no other garment underneath, black tights and white pumps. Ever an exhibitionist, she had offered to fight bare to the waist, but was advised this would offer the marshal a reason for banning the bout. On her hands were black six ounce gloves. These had been selected by her trainer, instead of the smaller variety she had used for practice, as being somewhat less damaging. He pointed out that it was likely her opponent would land at least some hits on her so that the precaution was worthwhile.

All in all, the red head was feeling a deep sense of satisfaction and little apprehension. After the earlier setbacks to her desire to regain control of the lucrative business lost by her husband, she was satisfied that everything was finally going her way. Nor, despite the buxom blonde having agreed to the bout far more readily than was anticipated, did she experience any anxiety. Regardless of how tough the other had proved since arriving, or even if she had some skill with boxing gloves, there were arrangements made to ensure she would be put at a disadvantage.

For her part, Madam Bulldog seemed just as much at ease. Like Wanda, she had had her hair bound back to form what a later generation would call a 'pony tail'. Albeit somewhat more demurely her attire was almost identical to that of the red head, although it was still far from being decorous and gave just as many indications that it was the only covering above the waist. Nothing of her thoughts showed, but she knew she was in for a rough time no matter what the result. However, she had overcome one pitfall placed in her path. The local medical practitioner had been prevented from acting as her second, but she had Marvin Eldridge 'Doc' Leroy assisting Greta Kusin. Having seen him attend to and, according to Connel, save the life of her servant, then deal with the wounds of the would be robbers, she had complete confidence in his ability to administer to her needs.

An expectant hush fell over the crowd as the doctor, clad in a black shirt, Levi pants and moccasins, called the women to join him at the centre of the ring. Although aware that trying to end the fight by awarding a disqualification would in all probability be futile, he told them what kind of conduct was or was not permissible. Then he ordered them to shake hands, return to their corners and come out fighting on the bell. Madam extended her right hand, but Wanda knocked it aside and walked away. Giving a shrug, the blonde returned to her corner.

Seated at the side of the ring, with a stop watch, brass gong and the two small bags containing the four thousand dollars 'purse' on his small table, Schanz was acting as timekeeper. Setting the watch for three minutes, he banged the gong with its brass hammer to signal the commencement of the round. Having had gum-shields slipped into their mouths, the two women began to cross to the centre of the ring. Studying Madam's posture, Wanda concluded she knew at least the basics of boxing. The summation was mutual, although the blonde had suspected such to be the case from the moment the challenge was uttered.

As the women converged in the centre, regardless of the way in which her offer to shake hands had been treated, instinct caused Madam to extend her gloves for the already accepted convention of touching those of her opponent to signify the commencement of the first round. Her sporting action was ignored, being greeted by a swift left jab to the face which jolted back her head. Angered by the violation of her sporting gesture, she could not prevent herself retaliating with a roundhouse swing of the right hand. It was, she realized just too late to halt the movement, ill advised.

Justifying the realisation, Wanda dodged the blow by bending at the waist and retaining her balance by keeping her feet in the places from which she had delivered the jab. Remaining in the crouch after the blow passed harmlessly over her head, she rammed her own right deep into Madam's unguarded navel. Although most of the air was driven from her lungs and her senses started to swim, instinct caused the blonde to collapse against and wrap her arms around the red head. Straightening from the evasion, Wanda was ensnared before she could get clear. Nor could she burst free of the embrace which was pinioning her arms.

'Break!' Connel ordered.

Having gained a brief and badly needed respite, Madam obeyed. Opening her arms suddenly, she thrust herself away in the hope of geting clear to manoeuvre. Aware of the chance she had made, Wanda threw a left hook to Madam's head with all her power. It was a blow which could have put her opponent in severe difficulty, but it failed to connect. Adequately recovered during the short clinch, the blonde avoided it and retaliated with a straight and jolting left to the jaw of the red head. Dazed by the blow, Wanda was wide open for the right cross which caught her nose. While it did not draw blood, it was sufficiently painful to cause her to cover up and retire across the ring.

Still feeling the effects of the body blow, Madam did not follow up on the advantage she had gained immediately. Instead, she concentrated upon replenishing her lungs despite knowing the other woman would also be recovering. This proved to be the case and, when they moved forward, they began to circle warily. Each was waiting, feeling the other out with probing left or right jabs, alert for any opportunity to initiate another telling and damaging attack. Remembering what she had been told, Wanda concentrated upon trying to keep her opponent facing the livery barn.

Having arrived early, to acquire the point of vantage selected by Good when the open air venue was organized, one of the contingent from Garnett had a small window to himself in the hay loft. Carrying out the instructions given by Wallace, to whom he had been sent by County Sheriff Lloyd Bowman, he slipped a small mirror from his jacket pocket. Having glanced around to make sure he was not observed, he began to direct the reflection from the afternoon sun towards the ring. After only a couple of attempts, he achieved his purpose.

Caught in the face by the unexpected glare, Madam was dazzled and she faltered in her movements. Alert for this, Wanda hurled a left hook upwards to catch her full beneath her jutting right breast. Gasping in pain, she stumbled backwards and desperately went into a protective crouch. Following her, the red head pounded at her shoulders and arms in an attempt to get through to her head. Herded into a corner, she managed to slip on to her knees and the referee ordered her assailant to move away. On the count reaching eight, the blonde regained her feet; but her eyes were still blinking and raw agony beat from the point she had been struck. Believing nothing other than a chance reflection from a window had caused her misfortune, she went warily to meet the eagerly approaching Wanda after her gloves had been wiped clean by Connel.

Having heard comments leading him to assume foul play was contemplated, while playing poker at the Barnhof Saloon the previous evening, Joseph Brambile had informed the other gamblers invited by Madam. They were positioned around the ring, alert for any eventuality. Seeing the flashing light and its aftermath, Poker Alice left her seat and headed for the livery barn. No man could have got through the crowd of spectators so quickly, but they made for the beautiful Englishwoman.

By the window, delighted with the success he had achieved, the man was waiting for another opportunity. Either by chance or design, the blonde did not present it so readily. However, at last the red head managed to bring her to face his position. He was preparing to align the mirror when something hard was pushed between his spread apart legs.

'Despite being raised a lady,' said a gentle feminine voice, yet chilling in its implied menace, to the accompaniment of the unmistakable sound of a firearm being cocked. 'I intend to try and blow your balls out of the top of your head if you so much as quiver!'

'Wha—Who—?' the man croaked, realizing there was every chance of the threat being put into effect.

'I'll take the mirror,' the speaker declared, reaching with her free hand to do so. Stepping swiftly beyond grabbing distance, she went on, 'Now light a shuck, as you colonials put it. If you're still around when Madam has thrashed that red haired *person* as soundly as she deserves, I would hate to be in your shoes.

Sidling away from Poker Alice, with his eyes fixed on the Remington Double Deringer she was holding, the man scuttled to the ladder by which he had gained admission to the loft and disappeared down it. Returning the pistol to her reticule, she took his place at the window. Watching Madam and Wanda continuing their boxing, a smile came to her face as she saw the chance she was seeking. Putting the mirror and sun to the same use, she had a different objective.

Affected by the light as the blonde had been, Wanda came off somewhat worse. She was caught first in the *solar plexus* by a solid left, then a right to the temple as she retreated, and she began to fold at the middle and go down onto her hands and knees. Shaking her head and gasping, she remained there for a count of eight. Still showing the effects as she regained her feet, she was saved from further punishment by the gong being

ounded by Schanz—slightly ahead of time—to bring
he round to an end.

'What the "something" happened?' the red head
demanded furiously, on reaching her corner and sit-
ing on the stool placed for her by Good. 'That bastard
n the loft blinded *me* the second time.'

'The stupid ba—!' Wallace began, gazing at the livery
arn. 'Hell's fire!'

'What's up?' Good growled, looking in the same
direction. 'Hot damn!'

Duplicating the action of her seconds, Wanda saw to
er consternation that Poker Alice was standing at the
window instead of the man from Garnett. After
waving it in admonition, the Englishwoman tossed the
mirror to the ground.

'That "mother-something" Limey's on to us!' the red
ead breathed.

'Don't worry,' Good replied. 'We've got other
hings's she can't get at and stop!'

* * *

'Hey, Marshal Collier!'

Hearing his named called in a young voice, the
peace officer turned his attention from discussing the
rst round with his deputy. Looking around, he
nodded a greeting to the fourteen year old son of the
mayor.

'Howdy, Billy. Why all the rush?'

'Momma's sent me to fetch you, daddy, the banker
nd Lawyer Scrope,' the boy replied.'Whee-dogie, is
he in a tizz?'

'Why'd that be?' Collier asked, always having re-
arded Mrs. Olivia Tyler as one of the more respons-
le members of the Ladies Guild For Civic Betterment.

'A deputy from Garnett's just fogged in,' Billy
xplained. 'Says he's been sent by the sheriff to tell us
tanton Howard's coming and'll hit town around four
'clock.'

'*Four*?' the marshal growled, taking out and consul
ing his watch. 'Hell, it's coming up to twenty to nov
Go get the mayor and the others, Pockets!'

'Well, isn't that the damned, all-fired most *awkwar*
thing?' Hebert Tyler declared, after the order wa
obeyed and the news delivered via Billy was passed o
by Collier. He jerked his head towards where th
second round was being commenced and continued
'We can't let Howard know this's going on!'

'There'll be a riot if it's stopped,' the marsh.
estimated grimly. 'Which we don't want him to se
either. What else did your momma say, Billy?'

'She'll have all the ladies waiting to meet him in th
Square,' the boy replied. 'And she reckons it'd be be
was you-all on hand's well.'

'Smart figuring,' Collier declared, deciding his con!
dence in the wife of the mayor had not been betraye
'We'll take him straight into the Fortescue Hotel an
that'll keep him out of the way until the fight's ove
Happen we're lucky, he'll not get to know what's bee
going on.'

CHAPTER SEVENTEEN

Fight Fire With Fire

'All right, god damn it, what's that "mother-something" son-of-a-bitch with the bean-shooter holding back for?' Wanda Higgins gasped, sinking tiredly on to the stool placed for her in the red corner by her seconds at the end of the sixth round. Pushing aside the wet sponge with which Stephen Good was preparing to wipe away the blood running from her swollen nose, she continued in a voice of close to breathless fury. 'I've had Bulldog against the ropes where he could have hit her at least half a dozen times, but he just sits on his fat ass like he was turned to stone.'

'Don't I know it?' Leo Wallace growled, the tirade having been directed chiefly towards him, applying a pad of cloth soaked in cold water to the badly puffed left eye of his half-sister with the intention of reducing, if not stopping, further swelling which would close it. Every time I look at the bastard, he just stares back like a sick cow!'

'Hey!' the trainer ejaculated. 'Madame Moustache's sat just behind him. Maybe it's something she's doing!'

As he was to discover later, Good had made an accurate summation!

However, putting aside thoughts on why another ploy intended to give an advantage to the red head was failing to materialize, the two men set about the task of reviving her as much as possible ready for when the gong was sounded to resume the fighting.

From the commencement of the second round, Wanda had been given further confirmation that she was in contention against a competent and dangerous opponent. One, moreover, possessing sufficient skill to offset the benefits the red head might otherwise have expected to accrue from her extra size, weight and length of reach. Therefore, it had been a bitter and closely contested fight with no quarter being offered or anticipated.

Many were the power packed punches traded by the two women!

Hooks, jabs, uppercuts, cross punches and even roundhouse swings were employed with complete impartiality, to be blocked, deflected, dodged, or accepted as was directed by ability and chance. Time after time, the hard packed six ounce boxing gloves made contact against the head, face, *solar plexus* and stomach, above the level of the tights; or below it when Wanda had seen a chance to do so without detection by Doctor Henry Connel. Although also against the rules, she had deliberately attacked the kidney region during clinches.

However, by far the worst suffering was being inflicted upon each bosom. Offered not the slightest protection by the mutually flimsy coverings, both sizeable pairs of breasts were assailed at every chance until the torment caused to the virtually unsupported mounds by unavoidable movements, as well as further blows, was close to purgatory. Between the rounds, inspections carried out upon their principals by Greta Kusin and Good had disclosed this most vulnerable portion of the feminine anatomy was becoming mottled by bruises, but the pain being caused was impossible to counteract and had to be endured.

On the other hand, the rest of the attentions given by both pairs of seconds had been efficacious. Nor had the anticipated advantage expected for Wanda, where such ministrations were concerned, materialized. Much to the surprise of Good in particular, the apparently strange selection of a male second by Madam Bulldog had proved more beneficial than his own in some respects. Making the most of a wide medical knowledge, including some primitive and yet effective methods, Marvin Eldridge 'Doc' Leroy had done much to help the blonde to commence each successive round in the best possible condition. Acting upon advice given by Connel that morning, he had also applied bandages to protect the knuckles as skilfully as those which had been expected to supply another advantage to her opponent.

Much to her growing consternation, following the removal of the man from the hay loft of Pegler's livery barn, the red head had had none of the promised illicit assistance from outside the ring. Instead, she had been compelled to depend upon the tricks taught to her as a matter of course by Good. These had not been confined to low and kidney punching. During clinches, she had stamped upon her opponent's feet, brought a knee up between the thighs, and tried to gouge the eye on the side away from the referee with her thumb. Nevertheless, she had discovered the blonde was conversant with and reduced the effectiveness of such methods. On three occasions, she had been seen in violation of the rules by Connel. However, aware that to award the fight to Madam Bulldog by a disqualification would have been disputed by Wanda's supporters and might easily end in a violent confrontation with those in favour of the winner, he had done no more than warn her against continuing to use such tactics.

Although the man to whom the red head had referred had been instructed to render assistance, distracting the blonde by blowing dried peas at her through a cigar holder improvising as a bean-shooter, he had been prevented from doing so.

Having decided on the methods which might be employed against their friend, the gamblers she had invited had combined their not inconsiderable knowledge to circumvent such attempts. Making an accurate deduction with regards to the cigar holder, Madame Moustache had employed her feminine charm to obtain a seat behind the man. At the first suggestion of her assumption being correct, she had intervened.

'*M'sieur*, do not try it!' the man had heard, in a husky feminine voice with a sensuous French accent—albeit, more menacing than sensual in the present circumstances—from his rear, while he was starting to remove the cigar from its holder, counting upon everybody around being too engrossed to detect him. 'I am holding a revolver in my reticule and, if you don't go on smoking, instead of what you've been told to do, I will most certainly put a bullet through your spine.'

Being unwilling to take the chance of the threat being carried out, the man had refrained from interfering and had settled down to enjoy the fight!

'Do something then!' Wanda demanded, glaring at the trainer. 'She's hurting the hell out of me!'

'There's one thing I could do,' Good replied. 'But it's not going to be easy for you!'

'What is it?' the red head asked and, on being told, went on, 'Do it and I'll take my chances.'

Reaching into the bag containing his medical and other equipment, the trainer took out a bottle filled with a reddish powder. Having dried the outside of the right glove, he tipped some of the contents upon its punching surface.

'There you are,' Good said and added a warning, 'You'll have to hold back with your right until you get a chance to shove the powder into her eyes or, if you can't get at them, her nose. It'll either blind her, or make her sneeze. Either way, you've got her!'

Time was sounded and the two women came out. Instantly, the red head found herself at a disadvantage as a result of the preparations made to put the blonde in serious difficulties. Wanting to use the red powder, she was compelled to keep the right away from any contact which would remove at least some of it from her glove. Depending solely upon the left for offensive purposes against a woman of her opponent's ability was far from satisfactory or safe. In fact, it led to the acceptance of so much punishment that she was tempted to forego the attempt as the seconds became first one and then two minutes without being granted an opportunity to capitalize upon it.

However, when the opportunity came, it seemed likely to justify the suffering and waiting.

Seeing her chance, Wanda threw the right glove towards Madam's momentarily unguarded face. Missing the intended target of the eyes, one of which was almost closed despite all the efforts of the seconds to prevent this, the contact was made on the nose. Twisting her hand to ram as much of the powder as possible into the nostrils, the red head went backwards a couple of steps. Having inadvertently breathed in on being struck, the blonde had helped to achieve the purpose of the attack. About to move towards her opponent, she felt a sensation of irritation in her nose. It twitched and a sneeze wracked her whole body.

Ready for such an eventuality, the red head literally sprang into the attack. Driving a left hook upwards into Madam's now undefended belly, Wanda folded her on to an uppercut from the right. Lifted erect, the blonde took a left cross to the side of the head. Pain erupted through her and, involuntarily spitting out the gum-shield, she was sent in a twirling plunge against the ropes. They halted her headlong rush and she crumpled in a mass of torment on to the canvas covered padded flanks which formed the floor of the ring.

Sorely stricken though she was, Madam might have counted herself fortunate in one respect. Due to the punishment absorbed while awaiting the opportunity to apply the powder, Wanda had not been able to put her earlier full power into the blows. If she had, the fight would have been over. As it was, the blonde retained just sufficient of her faculties to hear and realize what was meant by Connel starting to count.

However, knowing and doing something to remedy the situation were horses of a vastly different colour!

Listening to the words, 'One! Two! Three! Four!', Madam forced herself to think of the prize for which she was fighting. Somehow, calling upon what flagging energy remained, she managed to struggle to her feet and bring the count to a halt just as it reached nine. For all that, she had little control over her wobbly legs and her arms felt like lead as she raised them for Connel to wipe clean the gloves. Adding to her dilemma, she found herself being wracked by a second sneeze and knew another was forthcoming. Her condition, she concluded was far from capable of fending off whatever further attentions the red head might be planning to give to her.

All the audience and Wanda were equally aware of the blonde's precarious situation!

At his table by the ring, Rudolph Schanz took his gaze from the tottering owner of a rival saloon and turned it to his stopwatch!

The moving finger was just passing two minutes and thirty seconds!

In the first, third and fifth rounds, the saloon-keeper had sounded the gong early to relieve Wanda from difficulty. Now he could see he was presented with another opportunity to render another service. Given only a short period beyond the three minutes, she would be able to inflict further punishment, even if failing to attain a complete knockout.

There was only one fly in the ointment!

When the rest period after the fifth round was being taken, having written something in a notebook and torn out the page, Abraham 'Pappy' Maverick had risen and crossed to the table from his ringside seat. Under the pretense of inquiring whether there would be a game of poker at the Barnhof Saloon that evening he had slipped the paper into Schanz's hand. After the sixth round was started, the saloon-keeper had read what was written on it with a feeling of alarm and consternation.

'My watch is just as accurate as the one you're using. I start and stop it when you do. If you go under or over the three minutes just one more time, I will personally ram that gong up your butt and sound it with my gun butt.'

Repeated glances at the elderly gambler had revealed he was doing as promised. Having no doubt this was still the case, and fully aware of what would happen to him should the supporters of the blonde find out what he had already done—regardless of the threat from Maverick—he decided against doing anything which might give added assistance to the red head. There was, he told himself, just time for her to inflict further punishment legitimately before the three minutes were ended.

Much the same thought was passing through Wanda's head as she watched and waited impatiently to be able to resume the attack. However, the referee was still between her and her quarry. What was more, he was moving the blonde towards the blue corner instead of stepping aside and signalling for her to start fighting again.

Suspecting something illicit had been responsible for the sneezing, Connel had seen Wanda rubbing the right glove against the leg of her tights before he could check on whether he was correct in his assumption. He had noticed the holding back with that hand and remembered, too late to intervene, having heard a reason for such apparently pointless and even dangerous behaviour. Realizing that to make an accusation without proof would be construed as favouritism—or an attempt to save the blonde—by the supporters of the red head, he had seen a way he might gain her a badly needed respite. While making the count, he had retrieved a gum-shield. Now he was taking the legitimate action of arranging for it to be washed before allowing it to be replaced in Madam's mouth. Much to his satisfaction, the bell for the end of the round sounded before this could be done.

The next question, Connel told himself, was whether the blonde would be able to continue the fight.

The same thought was occurring to everybody else!

'The lousy bitch!' Madam gasped, half lying rather than sitting erect on the stool in the blue corner. However, so skilful had been the ministrations of her seconds, she was in better shape than she looked. Well enough, in fact, to be able to think clearly about how she had been treated during the final minute of the round. 'She had something that made me sneeze on her glove!'

'Why don't you tell the referee?' Greta suggested, glowering at the red head.

'It's too late to prove it now and they won't chance doing it again next round,' the blonde replied. 'She's been fouling me ever since we started. Now I'm going to fight fire with fire.'

A clang of the gong on the timekeeper's table signalled the commencement of the next round before any further explanation could be sought or supplied unasked!

Staggering from her corner, Madam moved in such a way that she looked much worse than she was feeling. However, her pose fooled Wanda. Advancing confidently, the red head decided she had nothing to fear and felt sure she could deal with the blonde in any way she fancied. Taking no precautions, she threw a jab towards the agony lined and bloody face of her opponent. Avoiding it, seemingly by accident, Madam went into a clinch. Clinging on and leaning all her weight against Wanda, she contrived to force them in a circle until she was in front of the referee and preventing him from seeing what she was contemplating. Hooking the thumbs of the gloves under the elasticated waist band of the red head's tights, she thrust downwards. Having done so, she liberated her hands so quickly nobody was aware of what she had done.

Even the red head failed to realize what had happened. Feeling the garment beginning an unaccountable downwards slide, she assumed the elastic had broken. Thrusting away her opponent, who went with surprisingly little opposition, she grabbed at the garment which was now a couple of inches below the bottom of her satin undershirt. Although the tights alone covered her nether regions, modesty had not provoked the action. She suspected that, on seeing they would not stay up, Connel would use it as an excuse to halt the fight at least until they could be replaced. That would allow time for the blonde to recover from the blows which had put her in such distress at the end of the previous round.

Just as Wanda was reaching these conclusions, Madam made the most of the opportunity she had created. Going back a short distance, she twisted to the left and lowered her near hand almost to the floor. Uncoiling to the right like a released spring, she brought the fist up in an arc with the whole weight and remaining power of her rotating body behind it. The glove struck the side of Wanda's jaw with terrific force. Her eyes glazed and closed, then her hands fell limply to her sides. Although she was knocked out on her feet, she was not allowed to fall without further attention from her opponent. Wanting to make sure there would be no return for the red head, the blonde slammed a straight right into her lower body. A left and right to each breast followed in rapid succession and, as their recipient's knees began to buckle, a left hook to the chin sent her over on to her back.

For a moment, staring down at the red head, Madam thought she had gone to far. Wanda lay absolutely motionless. Thinking the blows had killed her, it was with relief that the blonde saw her bosom start moving up and down. Although her arms were spread out, spasms affected her legs. It seemed she was trying to get up, bowing her body until it rested on her heels and shoulders. then a violent tremble ran through her and she subsided limply to the canvas once more.

The count was a mere formality!

Not even the most optimistic, or hopeful, spectator expected the red head to get up!

Nor did she!

Even as Madam's victory was being announced, men swarmed into the ring. Lifting her on to their shoulders, then thrusting the two bags of money forming the 'purse' into her still gloved hands, they carried her from the ring and in the direction of the Hide And Horn Saloon.

* * *

Triumphant though the arrival of Madam Bulldog in the square undoubtedly was, it could hardly have happened at a more inopportune moment in the estimation of some members of Tennyson's population!

Having made the journey from Garnett to Tennyson in a Rockaway road coach, County Sheriff Lloyd Bowman, although hearing the cheers and other sounds, was disappointed to discover that the fight was taking place where it could not be seen from Vernon Street or the Square. Nor, due to the competent way in which he was prevented by the respectable leaders of the town, had he managed to draw attention to the commotion and 'learn' what was causing it. Foiled in his purpose, he had derived what satisfaction he could from the small size of the party assembled to meet the man most favoured to be the next Governor of Texas. The welcome, he told himself, was nothing compared with what he had arranged to take place in the county seat.

However, if put out by the apparent lack of interest

in his visit, Stanton Howard had shown no trace of it. Tall, well built, distinguished looking—albeit with the rugged aura of one who enjoyed outdoor activities— he had greeted the few people assembled with an easy warmth and courtesy, as if a multitude and all the trimmings had been waiting for him.

Just as the introductions were concluded and Hubert Tyler was about to suggest going into the Fortescue Hotel, the first of the spectators emerged from the alley alongside the building carrying the victress on their shoulders. Coming to a halt at the sight of the distinguished looking group in the Square, they lowered her to the ground. Realizing something of civic importance must be taking place for the mayor, town marshal, banker and members of the Ladies Guild For Civic Betterment to have assembled, she was equally aware that she was far from presenting an appearance suitable for such an auspicious occasion.

Haggard from near exhaustion, Madam's battered and gory features were a clear indication that she had been indulging in a most unladylike activity. Speckled liberally with her own and Wanda Higgins' blood, the satin upper garment was so soaked by perspiration it emphasised rather than concealed the otherwise un-covered bosom beneath it and the tights had lost their knees on those occasions when she had been knocked to the canvas.

Looking in horror at the blonde, the 'good' women present began to mutter indignantly amongst them-selves. While relieved at the evidence that she had won the fight, Tyler, Collier, Scrope and the banker were all wishing she had delayed her return for just a couple more minutes. A smirk of delighted satisfaction came to the face of the sheriff at the possibilities he believed were now being presented. Like the promi-nent citizens of Tennyson, he watched for the effect that the sight would have on the distinguished visitor.

'My god!' Howard exclaimed, staring at the new arrivals. Then he walked forward saying in a tone of mingled warmth and concern, 'Well, Charlie, I'd heard you owned the saloon across yonder, and I meant to drop by for a noggin on the house. Great heavens, though, you look worse than when you and Russian Olga put on that bout of fisticuffs in aid of the Veteran's Home in San Francisco. What have you been up to this time?'

'I feel worse than I did then,' the blonde replied, thinking of her successful encounter with the claimant to be the champion female bare knuckle fighter of the world.[1] Glancing at the bags she was still carrying, she turned her gaze to the now puzzled group of women and advanced holding them out. 'Here you are, Mrs. Tyler. Put the purse for the bout to your fund for building a new schoolhouse, please.'

'O—Of course, Madam Bulldog,' the wife of the mayor assented, recovering her wits more quickly than any of her female companions. 'And thank you on behalf of us all.'

'May I make a suggestion, ladies and gentlemen?' Howard requested, and was given an almost unanimous concurrence. 'Providing Char—*Madam Bulldog* feels up to it, perhaps we might go into her place and drink to her success in this latest fistic encounter?'

'I'd be honoured and delighted to have you all as my guests,' the blonde declared. 'And I think you, ladies, may find some wine I have to your taste. Please come across, all of you.'

Walking towards the other side of the Square between Howard and Tyler, with the rest of the crowd following, not even the pain which wracked her whole being could prevent Madam feeling satisfied with her lot in life. Not only had she defeated a threat to her possession of a lucrative business, but she believed

1. *Information regarding some of the career of 'Russian Olga' Petrosky came be found in:* QUIET TOWN *and* TROUBLE TRAIL. *J.T.E.*

nothing of the kind would be attempted in the future.[2] Furthermore, aided by her friendship with Stanton Howard, the means used in the thwarted attempt to discredit her, had allowed her to make a vast improvement to her standing in the community. She felt sure that she would have no further trouble from the Ladies Guild For Civic Improvement and was confident she would retain the respect and companionship of those male members of the population who counted.

All in all, Madam Bulldog considered her future was now assured as the owner of the Hide And Horn Saloon.

2. *On hearing of the means intended to ensure victory for Wanda Higgins, Town Marshal Tune Collier had stated his intention of arresting her and the men responsible. Asked to refrain by Madam Bulldog, he had contented himself with ordering the red head and Leo Wallace to stay out of his bailiwick. Although he was unable to include Moses Stern in his ban, the other two obeyed his instructions. As we explain in;* CUT ONE, THEY ALL BLEED, *Wanda tried other means to dislodge Madam. She was unsuccessful and, following the events recorded in the sequel to this volume, gave up her hopes of doing so and left Garnett and Sand County for ever. J.T.E.*

APPENDIX

Throughout the years we have been writing, we have frequently received letters asking for various Western terms, or events we described, to be explained in greater detail. While we do not have the slightest objection to receiving such correspondence, we have found it saves much time consuming repetition to include those most often requested in each volume. We ask all our 'old chums', who have seen them before, to bear with us and remember there are always 'new chums' coming along who have not.

1. *'Gone to Texas'; at odds with the law, generally in the United States of America at the time the saying was brought into general usage. Many wanted men and fugitives from justice entered Texas during the colonization period—which had commenced in the early 1820's, due to the Mexican Government offering land for settlement to 'Anglos' so they would serve as a 'buffer state' against the depredations of marauding Indians—and continued until annexation as a State of the Union on February the 16th, 1846. Before that became a fact, such miscreants had known there was little danger of being arrested and extradited by the local authorities. Therefore, like Kenya from the mid-1920's until the outbreak of World War II—in spite of the great number of honest, law abiding and hard working folks who genuinely wished to make their homes there—Texas during the days before independence from Mexican domination was obtained had gained a reputation for being 'a place in the sun for shady people'.*

2. *Although the military sometimes claimed derisively that it was*

easier to kill a sailor than a soldier, the weight factor of the respective weapons caused the United States' Navy to adopt a revolver of .36 of an inch in calibre while the Army employed the heavier .44. The weapon could be carried on the belt of a seaman and not—handguns having originally and primarily been developed for use by cavalry—on the person or saddle of a man who did all his travelling and fighting on the back of a horse. Therefore, .44 became known as the 'Army' and .36 the 'Navy' calibre respectively. Colt 1860 Army Model revolvers intended primarily for sale to the military had barrels eight inches in length and those manufactured for the civilian market were half an inch shorter. However, when production was commenced on the legendary Colt Model P 'Single action Army' revolver in 1873—more detailed information about which can be found in those volumes of the Floating Outfit *series following* THE PEACEMAKERS *on the chronological list—it was made to accept a .45 calibre metallic cartridge.*

3. 'Light a shuck': cowhands' expression for leaving hurriedly. It derived from the habit in night camps of trail drives and roundups on the open range of supplying 'shucks'—dried corn cobs—to be lit and used as illumination by anybody who had to leave the fire and walk in the darkness. As the 'shuck' burned away quickly, a person had to move fast if wanting to benefit from the light. Information about the handling of a trail drive and the way in which an open range roundup was carried out can be found respectively in: TRAIL BOSS *and* THE MAN FROM TEXAS. *Incidentally, our original title for the latter was—in our opinion, but not that of the editor of our first publishers—the much more appropriate,* ROUNDUP CAPTAIN.

4. 'Up to the Green River': dependant on the context in which it is used, either to kill, or to give complete support. First produced at a factory on the Green River, at Green Field, Massachusetts, in 1834, a very popular brand of knife had the inscription, 'J. Russell & Co./Green River Works', on the blade just below the hilt. Therefore, any edged weapon thrust into an enemy 'up to the Green River' would almost certainly inflict a fatal wound whether it bore the inscription or not.

5. While on the subject of knives: a 'clip point' blade has the last few inches of the otherwise unsharpened 'back'—when laid in a horizontal position with the edge down and the handle to the left of

205

the viewer—joining and becoming an extension of the cutting surface in a concave arc. This is the characteristic feature of all 'bowie' knives. A 'spear point', which is less utilitarian and employed on pure fighting rather than general purpose knives, is formed by the two sharpened sides of the blade coming together in symmetrical curves. What happened to James Bowie's knife after his death in the final assault on the besieged Alamo Mission at San Antonio de Bexar, Texas, on March the 6th, 1836, is told in: GET URREA and THE QUEST FOR BOWIE'S BLADE.

6. We strongly suspect that the trend in film and television Westerns made since the early 1960's to portray all cowhands as long haired, heavily bearded and filthy stems less from the desire of the production companies to portray 'realism' than because there were so few actors—particularly to play supporting roles—who had short hair and were clean shaven. Another reason may be because the 'liberal' elements who were gaining control of the mass entertainment media appear to have obtained some form of ego trip by showing dirty habits, conditions and appearances. In our extensive reference library, we cannot find even a dozen photographs of actual cowhands—as opposed to Army scouts, mountain men and old time gold prospectors—with long hair and bushy beards. Nor did the great artists of the period show them in such a fashion. Furthermore, our reading on the subject and conversations with friends who live in the modern West have led us to assume the term, 'long hair', was one of opprobrium in the Old West and Prohibition eras, just as it still is in cattle raising country today.

7. 'Mason-Dixon' line, sometimes erroneously called the 'Mason-Dixie' line. The boundary between Pennsylvania and Maryland as surveyed in 1763-67 by the Englishmen, Charles Mason and Jeremiah Dixon. It became known as the dividing line between the Southern 'Slave' and the Northern 'Free' States.

8. 'Make wolf bait'; another term meaning to kill. It derived from the practise in the Old West, when a range was infested by stock destroying predators—not necessarily just wolves, but mountain lion, black or grizzly bears and coyotes—of slaughtering an animal and, having poisoned the carcase, leaving it where it fell to be devoured by the carnivores.

9. 'New England': the North East section of the United States, including Massachusetts, New Hampshire, Maine, Vermont, Con-

necticut and Rhode Island, which was first settled primarily by people from the British Isles.

10. In the Old West, the jurisdictional powers of the various types of law enforcement agencies were established as follows. A town marshal, sometimes called 'constable' in smaller places, and his deputies were confined to the town or city which appointed them. A sheriff and his deputies were elected by and confined to their county of origin. However, in less heavily populated areas, he might also serve as town marshal for the county seat. Texas and Arizona Rangers could go anywhere within the boundaries of their respective States, but were technically required to await an invitation by the local peace officers involved before participating in an investigation. As we explain in the Alvin Dustine 'Cap' Fog series, during the Prohibition era, Company 'Z' of the Texas Rangers were allowed to initiate operations without awaiting an invitation. Although a United States marshal and his deputies had jurisdiction everywhere in the country, their main function was the investigation of Federal crimes. Information regarding the duties, equipment and organization of a modern day sheriff's office in Texas can be found in the various volumes of the Rockabye County series.

11. Americans in general used the word 'cinch', derived from the Spanish, 'cincha', for the short band made from coarsely woven horsehair, canvas, or cordage and terminated at each end with a metal ring which—together with the latigo—is used to fasten the saddle on the back of a horse. However, because of its Mexican connotations, Texans employed the term 'girth' and generally pronounced it, 'girt'. As cowhands of the Lone Star State fastened the end of the lariat to the saddlehorn when roping half wild longhorn cattle, or free ranging mustangs, instead of using a 'dally' which could be slipped free almost instantaneously in an emergency, their saddles had two girths for added security.

12. 'Right as the Indian side of a horse': a saying derived from the habit of Indians of mounting from the right, or 'off' side instead of the 'near' or left as was done by Americans of European descent and Mexicans.

13. 'Summer name': an alias. In the Old West, a person could offer any name as a means of introduction. The only permissible way to express doubt without arousing hostility was to inquire, 'Is that your summer name?'

14. 'Pick up his toes': a cowhands' term for inflicting punishment. It derived from a throw with a lariat intended to catch a moving animal by the forefeet. Generally, the method was only employed to punish a horse which persisted in breaking out of the wrangler's rope corral when part of a remuda. While extremely dangerous to carry out, such a throw was used on a basis of 'kill or cure'. The other members of the remuda could pick up the habit if the offender was allowed to go unchecked. A description of how the throw was made and its effect is given in: TRAIL BOSS.